This is a work of fiction. The characters and events in this short story are products of the author's imagination and are fictitious. Any similarity to real persons, living or dead, or events is coincidental and not intended by the author. No part of this book may be used or reproduced in any manner whatsoever without the prior permission of the author, except by a reviewer who may quote brief passages in a review.

© 2017 Graeme Watson

Cover photograph by Graeme Watson

"Taking risks, surviving the unexpected, listening to inner voices, can be a doorway to a richer life. 'The Factory Challenge' is about a Canadian in the 1960s decides to follow this riskier path leading to a story of sudden surprises and transformation. Join the characters of this modern Canterbury tale on the road to oil exploration and spirituality."

"Changing technology and social direction brings unrest and opportunity. In 'Energized,' a struggling young man, who initially is a victim of such changes, seizes the chance to join the solar power movement. He renews his own life in the process. This optimistic story is also a lesson in Canadiana, faith, volunteering, and the power of relationships."

- Gary Bist, former teacher and technical writer at IBM

About the Author

Graeme works for the federal government at Library and Archives Canada, in the Access to Information and Privacy field. He worked the first half-decade of his career at Transport Canada, and has a Co-op Baccalaureate in International Development and Globalization, as well as a teacher's degree, both from the University of Ottawa. Graeme is married to Leslie, volunteers with Scouts Canada and is a member of the Gideons International in Canada. Graeme loves current events, biking, running and staying active whenever possible! He has a keen interest in most things Canadian. You can find out more about him and his books on his website, www.graemewatson86.com.

Acknowledgments

I would like to acknowledge the wonderful help and loving support of my dear wife Leslie, who helped me with this project. Also, I am appreciative for the encouragement of my faith-family at Celebration! Church in Ottawa. I am deeply grateful for Stacey Atkinson at Mirror Image Publishing, for her hard work in editing this manuscript. I am thankful for Gary Bist taking the time to review the manuscript.

Part I: The Factory Challenge

Chapter 1

Bob McConnell stood at his window with his morning coffee, gazing out at the tall buildings where once it was all farmland. He grew up on a farm not too far from Alliston, Ontario. Having attended a one-room schoolhouse, he graduated from grade thirteen, top of his class, an accomplishment of which he was extremely proud. His people had worked the land, lived and died on the land. But over time, a gradual disconnect had occurred between the people and the land.

The funeral was sombre. Bob's uncle Fred was busy telling about his father, Edward McConnell, who had died after a long battle with cancer. He was a hard-working man, but as he was pushing his midsixties, his beer belly was becoming all too obvious. Had it happened since he started using mechanized farming equipment?

"You know, the middle of the century ushered in a new era," Fred told the small group gathered around the casket. "Gone are the days when the majority of Canadians grew up on farms, worked on farms and died on farms, along with all their other siblings. Henry Ford's factory changed everything. Now, the drive of the economy is in large part thanks to modern machinery and equipment. Just look at all those huge office towers at the corners of the bustling metropolitan areas of Montreal, Toronto, Vancouver and Winnipeg, looming over the landscape. The Cold War's in full swing. Taylor's scientific management ideas have taken over."

Fred was clearly a formidable storyteller, and a successful farmer at that. Bob's father, on the other hand, was not as successful and did not work as hard as his younger brother. Sadly, Edward had to sell off bits and pieces of his farm over the years in an effort to stay afloat financially.

Bob was the second youngest of ten children, and growing up he had to find a way of escape. He was determined to not let circumstance dictate his destiny. He was determined to break the mould. Do something different. Something that would make his family proud.

After high school, he had ventured off to the Second World War, as so many other young men were doing. Was it a way of escape? For a sense of adventure? To leave familial obligations behind? The foremost reason was for a sense of adventure—a yearning—and to preserve the ideals of Western democracy against the atrocities of Hitler fascism, a cause which bolstered the Allied forces.

He remembered the day, clear as a whistle, when he left everything that he knew behind to serve his country. Perhaps it was more accurate to say that he was serving the Queen of England, but nevertheless, it was in the interests of Canada. He could still smell the steam from the large ship and picture it as it set off from Halifax, sending him, along with all of his fellow compatriots, off to war. Bob would not return for another six whole years.

Serving in the Second World War reminded him of the sacrifice of his father and other relatives who had served in the First World War, the War of 1812 and the 1837–1838 rebellion in Upper Canada, incited by the stalwart William Lyon Mackenzie. It seemed as if it were a ritual that men did, when they were a certain age, before getting married and having children—going off to war. It was a noble cause; albeit a societal necessity at times. South of the border, his wife's ancestors had proudly fought as Yanks in the American Civil War. Those forefathers fervently believed in emancipating the black man from the chains of slavery.

Bob would return from overseas married to a lovely young lass, Martha, born in the poor ghetto in Aberdeen, not too far away from the shipyards. His wife had served in the Women's Auxiliary Air Force. Great Britain war brides were quite common among the men of the Commonwealth who had served overseas. He had only courted her three short months before getting married! To think…that was unheard of today. The two of them had had a hard enough time finding a minister or priest who would marry them, especially considering Martha's father was fiercely opposed to the marriage.

But here they were, all of these years gone by and four children later, Bob knee-deep in a successful career in investment banking. The industry had undergone a definite transformation since the crash of 1929 and the Great Depression. Everyone was far more conservative. Speculation decreased. Greedy stockbrokers were eliminated from the banking industry. Many people invested in bonds or simply tucked their money safely away in savings accounts, which had comfortable enough interest rates. Even putting money under the mattress was not uncommon.

Fred McConnell had finally got off his soapbox and let the preacher give the eulogy.

"Edward McConnell, a First World War vet, always had high hopes for each one of his children. He wanted his sons to be prosperous. That was his dream. Something shared by most fathers." Father Sanders paused for effect.

Bob had a flashback as he considered how his father had always prodded him into pursuing a different career than the one Bob had decided upon. Surely, investment banking couldn't be a worthy choice, and true to his strict Methodist background, Edward McConnell also believed that all money was evil. It was never spoken about at home. Not a word, which might explain why Edward wasn't very good with money.

"Edward thought that a career involving your hands—building homes or office buildings, for example—was the most valuable profession," the father said, supressing a chuckle. "While a few of his children chose such careers, not all of them did…but all of his children have achieved a measure of success.

"McConnell believed that our modern society needed workers to get *real* things done. Concrete projects. Not people speculating on prices of precious metals or the latest trend that the Canadian economy would follow…there were far too many 'paper-pushers' out there. As far as Edward was concerned, he couldn't trust anyone but himself to handle his cash—not even his wife." By now there were a few snickers from the funeral attendees.

Bob felt he was being addressed directly. As a natural people-pleaser, he desired to live up to his father's expectations. On the other hand, he remembered how growing up he couldn't wait to escape the family farm and strike out on his own.

Bob sat back, grief-stricken, and reading the evening newspaper after his father's the funeral, in quiet reflection about the more positive experiences he's had with his father, like when they would fish at the stream near his homestead. The children were playing with their Tinkertoys, without a care in the world. Oh, to be young again! he thought. He was thankful he had settled with the banking profession. He counted his blessings. Many of his compatriots hadn't even made it home to see their families after the war. The men who grew up in his generation were duly recognized for their many heroic feats. They were a tougher breed synonymous with the biggest baby boom in Canadian history—a precursor to the massive expansion of the federal government during the Trudeau era. They witnessed the transformation from a rural, agrarian society to one predominately comprised of workers who clocked in their forty hours a week and came home to their suburban palace at the end of the day…only to repeat the same routine again the next morning.

Chapter 2

The puffs of smoke produced by the investment bankers at Ross Henry Bruckenheimmer LLP was not unlike what you would see in the offices of any major newspaper in Toronto the Good, as the city was known as at the time.

Surveying the scene of the Bay Street office, you saw men with their feet up on the desks, talking loudly on the phone to anyone remotely interested in being a prospective client. It was a dog-eat-dog world out there, and the investment bank that faired best employed the best salespeople. Those who impressed clients enough to have them fork over their life savings to these sometimes nefarious institutions not only survived but thrived.

Bob had steadily worked his way up to a cushy midmanagement-level position in the company. He had achieved this seniority through scrupulous study and coursework on the side, when he had joined the firm after returning from the war in 1945. Now, over fifteen years into his career, he was halfway to the top. Was there any other way to live your life? He could almost smell the success that awaited him. He would one day be president and CEO.

***

Bob's father had wanted him to do something "practical" with his hands, like building homes. The thought occurred to him, as he went outside to pick up his morning newspaper, that growing up, he wanted to do the exact opposite of what his father suggested he do. Although eventually, Bob became interested in real estate as a hobby, a way to make extra cash on the side. Bob was driven by the rush of making cold, hard cash.

In his spare time, Bob was building a mini-real-estate empire of his own. He successfully rented out multiple rooms in his boarding house. Now, he was getting into the market of brokering second mortgages. And he was making a killing at it!

Bob picked up the morning paper and got splashed by the first hint of rain. It donned on him how grateful he was for his wife's demobilization pay, which had covered the down payment for their home. It was a real fixer-upper, though. When they first moved in eight years ago, the roof leaked, the wood floors were badly in need of work and the whole place had to be painted. Although home renovations were not his forte, Bob recruited some of his younger friends to help him with the grunt work of getting the house presentable.

He scanned the Classifieds after completing a crossword in record time. Not bad for an amateur! He saw the ads for a couple of his rooms in his home, which he had been trying to rent now for a couple of months. Thankfully, he had received a few queries about them and was going to contact the interested parties later in the day.

"Did you take out the trash, Paul?" Bob asked.

"Not yet…" Paul muttered.

Bob wasn't afraid to get his children working young, even at eight years old. There wasn't going to be a McConnell with idle hands in his house!

***

The next day, Paul, the youngest child, was artfully building pretend structures in the sandbox, using sand wet from the watering can. During an unusually warm April, the sun was shining, and it seemed like the McConnell family hadn't a care in the world.

Bob McConnell arrived home early from his job. He had been labouring steadily for weeks at this one particular deal and was elated when it finally came to pass. Bob collapsed on the sofa when he entered his home. This was rather uncouth as his wife had just had it reupholstered last week. He had been thinking on the drive home about how Eisenhower's use of the term *military-industrial complex* couldn't be a more apt description of the direction the North American economy was headed. Bob's well-to-do patrons were shelling over large amounts of money, and he found himself investing it more and more into equipment that was supposedly protecting the continent from the Red Soviets.

Some of his wealthiest clients were lawyers who entrusted him with thousands of dollars in savings. These were the elites—the Toronto ruling class—a group of people that understood the unwritten rules of the wealthy, who talked big talks, walked big walks and were always abuzz with new ideas and ventures. The aristocratic class, as it were, had descended from generations of rich

Toronto merchants and businessmen; they were a highly cloistered, upper-crust group indeed. Insular, arranged marriages were commonplace, and the bourgeoisie liked to stay within the confines of their upper social strata.

"What's for dinner, lovie?" Bob said as he poked his balding head up from the sofa and threw his fedora onto the hook, narrowly missing two of his children's heads. The girls were playing with their recently acquired doll set, and the boys were running around the house playing cops and robbers.

"A little of this and a little of that." Martha gave him a peck on the cheek.

"I smell chicken," he grinned.

"Anyway, what's wrong with 'a little of this and a little of that?'" she said, defending herself.

They lived on Indian Park Road, a beautiful street in Toronto that went up and down and all around. Most importantly, it was near High Park, a wonderful diversion for the children, especially the eldest child, Rob, who enjoyed long days in the summer playing tennis.

Eventually, everyone gathered around the dinner table, as was part of their daily routine. In the general hubbub of the supper table, the family engaged in little banter. This was despite the fact that Bob, as a smart and educated man, had taught his family to discuss the day's events over dinner, but tonight there just simply wasn't much to talk about.

After dinner, Bob retreated to his study. He balanced his chequebook and knew where every dime of his family's monthly income went. Every piece of clothing was accounted for. He also spent some time investigating a new second mortgage his agent had given him as a referral.

Bob's daughters, Lois and Kathy, had piano lessons that evening, and Rob had his paper route, which kept all three busy after supper. Paul, meanwhile, moved indoors to play with his Tinkertoys in the living room.

As he was writing a few cheques, Bob was filled with gratitude that he could afford putting a couple of his children through piano lessons, and he was appreciative of the work ethic that the paper route taught his sixteen-year-old boy. Soon, though, Rob would start his job at "the big D" Dominion grocer. That job had great pay, flexible part-time hours and was the place that all Rob's buddies worked at. Being a part of a unionized company paid off, literally. Rob's other burgeoning passion was the Air Cadets, a program that he had joined recently, and was trying to squeeze in as much as possible in his hectic schedule.

In his study, examining his books, Bob felt wistfully reminiscent and thought back to his early days on the family farm. The whole agricultural process had undergone a profound evolution in the twentieth century. The early days were characterized by horse-and-buggy as the principle means of transport. Horses helped with farming activities: tilling, sowing and harvesting. They were invaluable. Now, the age of the automobile was also a time of major technological advances in the way of farming machinery. The modern tractor assisted farmers in efficiently harvesting their crops, and other tools, such as the combine harvester, allowed farmers to more easily collect and separate grain from the chaff, as well as to gather up straw or hay for use around the farm.

Bob found himself caught up in an internal dialogue. Had our modern society *really* benefited from all of these advances? Less people, such as family members, were required to complete the jobs around the farm. Farms grew to be bigger and bigger so that they could be profitable—often the farms would be a couple hundred acres. Another concurrent development in farming practice was monoculture . There were fewer subsistence farms and more farms that specialized in growing solely cash crops like wheat or soybeans or corn, to the exclusion of other crops or livestock.

As Bob completed his finances for the evening, he reasoned that another element that came with the supposed advancement in farming was the greater use of pesticides and insecticides. In fact, this was a major part of the *green revolution*. Chemically composed fertilizers, along with certain strains of seeds, were being used to greatly increase the farm yields. But again, at what cost? Would cancer rates increase? What other long-term health effects could these changes in agricultural practice produce?

Heading back downstairs for a spot of tea, Bob wagered that as a reaction to all of these modern developments, organic farming would soon be taking off. But not quite yet…monoculture was in, and suburbanization was in full swing. The baby boom was at its climax.

Bedroom communities all around North America were springing up. Simultaneously, the inner-city ghetto was emerging.

"Do you think that the hollowing out of our cities would contribute to greater crime in metropolitan areas?" Bob posited to his wife, taking a sip of tea.

Bob waited for an answer that did not come immediately. Bob's curiosity was getting the better of him. He truly questioned if he wanted to continue in his career as an investment banker. Maybe he should jump headlong into real estate? He had always fantasized about becoming CEO of Bruckenheimmer, but what about if he ventured out on his own and started on a brand new endeavour? The thought sent a thrill of excitement through him, along with fear. The stakes were high…if Bob failed, he would likely lose his house and maybe even his family!

Chapter 3

After several weeks of careful thought, Bob decided to venture out on his own, full time, into real estate. He had a piece of land in mind; it was near where his brother lived, north of Toronto, at the intersection of Yonge and Steeles.

The city of Toronto hadn't really grown that far yet, but Bob was hoping to buck that trend. He wagered that Toronto was going to keep expanding—northward, southward, eastward and westward. And Bob wanted to cash in on it.

But for now, he was going to use his nest egg—money he had collected from renting and from brokering second mortgages, as well as his personal saving—to purchase a tract of land and develop it commercially. The size of the land was twenty acres, and the price was incredible—only $30,000!

Now, the hard part. Bob had to give his resignation to a company that he'd committed his life to for the past fifteen years, and it wasn't going to be easy. Nevertheless, it had to be done.

Bob had spoken to Martha the night before. Surprisingly, she wasn't caught off guard by his decision, although she did put up a bit of a fight before agreeing to the decision. The terms were that Bob couldn't give up on being a residential landlord and brokering second mortgages on the side. That was a staple for the family. Bob had acquired a good deal of experience in these areas, and the McConnells began to rely on the steady stream of cash flow it produced.

At precisely nine o'clock on Monday morning, Bob walked into his fifty-storey office building, pushing through the rotating glass doors and moving slowly to the elevators. He was in no rush today.

"How about those Maple Leafs," Bob commented to a colleague, as he lit up a cigarette in the elevator. He shouldn't really have lighted up there, but he figured with two weeks left, what could he lose? It was nearing the end of the playoffs, and the Leafs were consistently winning against the Chicago Blackhawks.

"I think they have a mighty fine chance at winning the Cup," offered his colleague, Joe Mittal. He had a thick black moustache and salt and pepper hair that was carefully slicked back with Brylcreem. He was pushing fifty-five and looking forward to retirement.

Joe got off on the twenty-third floor, and then Bob got off a couple of floors after him. Bob shuffled to his office, which had been nearing the C-suite, until he had been convinced that he wanted to strike out on his own.

The nine-thirty meeting of firm associates was put off until ten due to an urgency that had sprung up. Mildly relieved, Bob took off his jacket, adjusted his suspenders and bow tie and sat down as comfortably as he could in his wooden chair.

He debated how much he needed to prepare for the upcoming meeting. Did he really care how he left his company when he would be striking out on his own in a short amount of time? The idea of going solo in business was so appealing.

After scribbling a few notes, Bob flipped to a new page and scribbled down some ideas about the company he hoped to start. As he was doing so, he wondered if it actually made sense to go it alone in his new venture. It was not that he didn't have the money, or was incapable of handling the stress, but Bob figured it made sense to have at least one wingman.

For a fleeting moment, Bob thought about Joe from the elevator. Although Joe would be a responsible sidekick, it struck Bob from previous conversations in social settings that Joe had no interest in going into business for himself. He was too into his hobbies—cooking, gardening and collecting antique motorcycles—to be of any use in making money in a small enterprise.

Bob scratched Joe's name off his list and considered a couple of other coworkers who exhibited initiative, creativity and general enthusiasm. He still couldn't place his finger on who might be a good fit.

Finally, as ten o'clock approached, Bob thought about his neighbour, Gordon. He was a reliable man, probably in his early sixties. His children had all grown up, and he found himself with increasingly freer time. He was a technical guy, a tradesman who specialized in repairing heavy machinery. Every night when Bob came home from work, he would see Gord faithfully working on some piece of equipment in his driveway.

That's it, Bob thought to himself. He was going to give Gord a try. The team of one was soon to, hopefully, become a winning pair.

***

Surprisingly, giving his boss his two weeks' notice was not difficult for Bob. John Vizant, his director, had half-expected him to be asking for a promotion.

"We've been looking the last few months to cut some slack in our budget," joked John. Bob smiled in response but thought about how insensitive his boss was acting. Didn't he wish Bob well in the new endeavour?

Bob had given the standard two weeks' notice, cognizant of the fact that some people would have given more time to their employer to allow them to find someone to take over the job. Frankly, Bob didn't care. While his company had paid him a decent salary, he knew he was replaceable. And John was serious, given the current market, when he said the company needed to find money from cutbacks.

When he got back to his desk, Bob started to clean up his belongings, which wasn't too much. He was a minimalist and hadn't kept a lot over the years. He gave his desk a good cleaning and started composing a final goodbye email to his unit, wishing everyone a fond farewell. The email wouldn't get sent, of course, until his final day, but Bob wanted to be organized and ready for a couple of Fridays from now, his last day of work.

***

After work, Bob excitedly drove to the soon-to-be location of his future business enterprise. He had tried a couple of times contacting the realtor, whose name was plastered on the big wooden placard advertising the land. The second time, he left his contact information with a lovely secretary who assured Bob that the realtor would get in touch with him. That was several days ago.

Bob found a place to park his station wagon and got out to survey the scene again. What he saw was a wheat field, surrounded by active farms, especially to the north. But it didn't take much of a stretch of imagination to picture major development here. Could buses and other transit, other than the automobile, come this far north of Toronto?

The stench of cow manure permeated the air. It was a hot day, and Bob's pores were opening up with the humid air as he felt a drip of sweat forming along his brow.

Nevertheless, Bob was placing his bets on expansive urban development in this neck of the woods. Bob got in his car and fired up the engine. It was a red Studebaker Wagonaire, a well-made, practical vehicle that suited Bob's penchant for buying quality goods that would last.

The urban growth (or sprawl, as the pessimists referred to it) wouldn't happen overnight, but sooner or later Toronto would mushroom, and its extremities would be linked to its core with a world-class subway system. He could visualize it already!

Bob merged onto Yonge Street. In the meantime, the age of the automobile had killed a lot of the push for public transit. Toronto's streetcars were barely holding on. Urban planning expert Jane Jacobs had it right when she envisioned "green" cities. That would be the way of the future.

Sitting in traffic, Bob reckoned that he had put in his time with the daily grind. He was done with eking out an existence by serving the mass of elites of the downtown Toronto establishment. It was time to start something new, to part with conventional wisdom. Time for a fresh start! He was going to make it out there, and he was going to make it big.

The next day before work, Bob got a call from the real estate agent about the land. How exciting!

Bob was at home for a bit before meeting up with a client, an elderly woman—Shauna Hannessy—a few doors down. He took a sip of hot coffee. He needed the caffeine. The excitement of his new venture kept him from sleeping last night.

"You got a bidding war on your hands," Don Trimmer, the realtor explained. On the other end, Don was blowing smoke ringlets in the air.

"I've never heard of that before!" Bob said, with incredulity. "I thought Canada had enough land to go around for everyone, as long as you worked hard and you earned your keep."

"I'm not denying *that*…" Don's voice sounded faint as he tried to gather his thoughts. "It's just that the particular plot you're looking at is hotly contested!"

"All right, I gotta go to another meeting. We'll talk later."

After work that day, Bob had a good, long conversation with his wife over dinner.

"Just be careful, sweetheart. Don't be foolish…if the price it too high, you can just say no. They'll be other opportunities…and you may want to reconsider resigning."

It was too late for that—he'd already given his notice. There was no turning back. Plus, Bob was determined to strike out on his own, no matter the odds against him.

Martha suppressed a tear. It was as if her family were on the brink of poverty, which simply wasn't the case.

Bob, taking a spoonful of soup determinedly, defended his decision. "You don't understand, Martha. I've done my research. This land is the cat's meow! I'm convinced it's the right decision. We *need* to buy it. Johnny Carruthers, the slime bucket developer whose stomping ground is about a mile south of the land, is visiting the site all the time, I saw him twice already there in the last week! Fortunately, he didn't see me…but the point is that a plot like that won't come up again that easy. The developers I'm trying to compete against are land-grabbing hogs."

Martha gave him a disgusted look. The message she conveyed said she needed more convincing.

Chapter 4

With just under two weeks left at work, Bob still had projects to finish up. He wanted to leave the job on good terms, hopefully with a reference, and make the transition for the colleague taking over his work as smooth as possible. I've had enough of meetings though, he thought, as he returned from one and began preparing for another in a half hour…there was no end in sight!

Some employees were grateful for Bob's departure because it meant that they could shore up clients without having to do too much legwork. Other employees, who already were swamped with their own caseloads, were anxious that they would not have the time to take on new accounts.

One particular juicy account that Bob actually enjoyed working on and had to wrap up involved raising capital for a large mining corporation, Xantratex, near Sudbury. This complicated account involved raising capital and issuing Class A and B shares for the client. Shareholders were being led by business magnate Regg Gardner and were pushing for a fairer valuation of the company as well as greater distribution of profits. This particular firm, under CEO Bernie Stomp, had a history of not treating its shareholders honestly, swindling and nickel-and-diming every investor in the company.

Bob had met with the Xantratex executives last month. The meeting, held in the prestigious Ross Henry boardroom, was mainly unproductive, with both major shareholders and company management at an impasse about what was considered *fair treatment*. The company had recently gone public and now was trying to rejig profit distributions to its benefit by splitting the shares. The meeting ended on a rather sour note, with management essentially dictating to the shareholders what their terms will be, as far as going public and splitting the shares was concerned.

Another account that was being transferred, this one to a more senior employee, consisted of advising a law firm client on the purchase of a medium-sized sawmill operation just outside of Yellowknife, Northwest Territories. An American multinational company, Cook Lafleche Holdings, had drafted up an agreement to purchase the operation. The sawmill, Bourgand Mill Ltd., was increasingly becoming profitable but could not expand without a massive injection of capital. The American corporation was happy to acquiesce to this, enthralled with the notion of expanding into Canada's North.

***

"We'll fork over the cash, but we wanna deal," Benny Dawson said, emphatically.

Dawson had worked for years on a thousand acre ranch in southeast Texas before defecting to the oil industry for two decades and then heading up a highly sought after investment firm, Cook Lafleche Holdings.

"We gotta have the right deal," said Bob, unswervingly, "And right now nothing's finalized. My client needs to know that this deal is as generous as possible, and I don't think it is. We're hoping for a five-hundred-thousand purchase price. Do you have any idea how much product this company has been churning out? I understand that nearly a third of all furniture manufactured in the North is made using Bourgand Mill's wood!"

"All right, well, I've got to take a client to lunch right now. Call me when you've got a slightly lower price."

"Benny, let me level with you. I'm striking out soon."

"Really?"

"Yeah…I just wanna get this account in order for the next guy."

"Okay, but whoever's fillin' your shoes better have thick skin!" Dawson took a swig of whiskey and then the phone clicked.

***

When Bob pulled into his driveway that evening, his friendly neighbour, Gord, was hard at work repairing his lawnmower.

"Hiya, neighbour!" Gord said enthusiastically.

It had been a long day for Bob. "Howdy," he managed.

They stood around chatting for a few minutes, and Bob mentioned that he was leaving his job and that some of his investment accounts were being transferred to his coworkers since he was striking out on his own.

"Ya know, I've got this sawmill case up north I'm trying to tie up desperately."

"Is it near Great Slave Lake?"

"You bet, just a few miles from it."

Gord tried to think about which company Bob might be referring to, given that there were only a handful of those companies up in that region. After a few minutes of guessing, Gord realized the futility since Bob couldn't divulge the confidentiality of his client.

After a short while, Bob quickly got straight down to business and explained to Gord about his entrepreneurial dream. Gord was more reluctant than Bob thought he'd be to join him in the real estate pursuit.

"I'll give it some thought, Bob," he said, giving the impression that he wasn't too excited. "I'll think about it and get back to you. By the way, this guy Carruthers keeps bugging me—he somehow got my number. He's interested in the property and doesn't to want to stop at anything to get it."

After Bob's Saturday morning run, he saw Gord again, this time cleaning the gutters of his home. Gord always keeps himself hard at work, thought Bob. A great characteristic to have in a business partner.

Bob went inside to shower and get dressed, and then he went out again to see Gord and invite him to his house for coffee. They started off again talking about the North, similar to their last exchange. Bob discovered that Gord was born in Fort Smith, Northwest Territories, and that he came from a long line of coal miners, explorers and *coureurs de bois* who had settled in that part of the country after the Klondike gold rush at the turn of the century. Gord talked about how his wife's Acadian family were also early settlers in Canada, having made their living primarily as cod fishermen on the east coast of the country.

Bob couldn't really comment anymore on life in the North, apart from his one business trip up there. He did mention, however, that Martha's father was a logger who hailed from Hay River and had an uncle from Aklavik, and that she, too, had come with Bob on the trip to the territory so that she could visit her family.

Eventually, the conversation turned to the subject of the real estate endeavour that Bob was excited about starting.

"Gord, did you have the opportunity to think things over and decide whether my business idea would be of interest to you?"

"I certainly did, Bob. And more importantly, I ran it by my wife. She thought it was a fantastic idea. We've decided that I could do it, as long as it starts out as a side project. If it proves profitable enough, I can go full time. My wife's retired, so we have a little bit of money coming in from her pension. But other than that, I still need a steady stream of income to cover our bills."

Bob took a sip of coffee and nodded his head. He understood. Although he was a lot more comfortable financially than his neighbour, he knew that starting a business was always a risky endeavour. Thankfully, he had his house paid off and was armed with what he felt to be the requisite experience to make his company profitable.

"I hear ya, buddy," Bob concurred.

***

There it was. A gorgeous, Victorian-era farmhouse that Martha had fallen in love with, located right outside of Georgetown, Ontario. It was the type the floors creaked when you walked on them. The house sat on a parcel of land that was roughly one hundred acres. Just big enough to be a great hobby farm, but a little too small to make a living off of the land.

After church on Sunday, Bob, Martha and the children had driven northwest of Toronto for an hour after getting a lead on a couple of beautiful properties. Martha's good friend from the sewing club knew about all the hot Toronto real estate deals. Her husband used to be a real estate agent and kept her abreast of the latest and greatest developments. And since Bob was going to take the plunge and start his own business, Martha was uneasy about the idea of moving.

Bob had actually preferred the Edwardian country home they had just viewed, outside of Milton. But after all, it was Martha who would be spending the most time at home, with the children. Thus, she held veto power when it came the selection of the McConnell residence.

The family had the unique opportunity of getting acquainted with the sellers of the home. They were a couple without children,

George and Dot, who had inherited the farm from a relative. They were aging and couldn't keep up with managing the property.

The price was right. Plus, Bob and Martha would make a substantial profit from the sale of their home in Rosedale and would easily be able to purchase this farmhouse while still having money to sock away in the bank after the realtor's fees and the moving expenses were covered.

The Georgetown home did require substantial work for it to be comfortably livable. But with all of the children chipping in, and Martha's hard work ethic, Bob was convinced that his family had a bright future in this neck of the woods.

Chapter 5

At the start of his final week of work, Bob called back the realtor for the land, eager that Carruthers hadn't snagged the property.

"That's okay. We have another client offering thirty-three thousand dollars... do you have an offer more generous than that?," said Don Trimmer, the agent.

Bob countered the offer with a slightly higher $35,000, which was going to be his final offer. Don accepted the deal as he had an instinctual feeling that Bob was more trustworthy than the other offer, coming from Carruthers. The two of them arranged to meet over lunch and get the offer signed as quickly as possible. Bob sighed with relief when he held the signed papers in his hand, and was glad to have this stressful deal out of the way. There would surely be other challenges with the building of the property and getting cash flow for his fledgling company, but at least the initial land purchase was soon to be out of the way.

Bob returned to his office and didn't have much to do, so he began sorting through several filing cabinets filled with client accounts, only half of which were redistributed around the firm.

Although, technically, Bob was a manager, he didn't do much managing at all. The firm always had so much work to go around that he was more of a mentor to his junior associates. He answered any questions they had, kept track of their attendance and vacation, shared his extensive experience with them and took care of minor disciplinary measures, if needed.

At the present time, he had one more account left that would take up most of his time before leaving his job. It was a merger of two Quebec-based companies. One was a manufacturer of airplanes, and the other made helicopters. Both sides had shareholders unwilling to budge with their share prices and corporate integration. Bob found that Ross Henry was more of a negotiator in this case, and an honest broker between the parties. Of course, similar to other cases, the lawyers were also getting involved, as they had their "legal expertise" to add, and ensured the companies complied with due diligence. But Bob found the attorneys to be more demanding financially for the deal than the investment bankers, and that's saying a lot! It was the investment bankers, though, who managed the more complicated side of the deal than the attorneys, such as how shareholders would vote, company valuation and the integration of the two record-keeping systems.

***

After work, Bob got around to meeting the other real estate agent, who was selling the farmhouse. There were so many details that needed to be settled: selling their old house, packing up their belongings, thinking about what needed fixing in the new house.

The purchase would be contingent on the sale of the McConnells' house in Toronto. Bob was sure that wouldn't be a problem. The market was hot. And the weather was getting warmer, too! Moving season was right around the corner.

Bob's last Wednesday at work was the day of the farewell lunch. The whole office attended; Bob was appreciated by everyone. Having been a fixture of the institution, there wasn't a single employee who doubted how much time and energy he had expended at the company over the years.

In an unexpected display of generosity, management arranged for a catered buffet. There were hors d'oeuvres and wine and plenty of speeches to go around.

At the climax of the luncheon, the senior vice-president of the firm—Dan Schmidt—gave a heartwarming but brief speech on behalf of the firm.

"I want to take this time to honour Mr. Bob Joseph McConnell. What a dedicated employee. He cared for each and every one of his team members. He saw his caseload through, from start to finish. If ever his projects faced challenging times, and they did, Bob never hesitated to go the extra mile and get the job done. Bob, you will be missed. We all know you are a very capable man and that you can accomplish whatever you set your mind to. All the best in the years to come. Just don't bite off more than you can chew!" With that, there was some stifled laughter and a gentle applause.

Then Dan gave a toast in honour of Bob, and all present raised a glass to celebrate his achievements. Also, Bob was given a few kitschy gifts, including some flowers and a pen with the name of Ross Henry emblazoned on it. Filled with gratitude, Bob thanked everyone, both from the front of the room and individually for their kind words and warm wishes.

The following Friday, the conditions of the McConnells' home sale and purchase had been met. Bob packed up and brought home his last box from work. Now, Saturday morning, moving day had arrived, and he was overseeing the transportation of his family's belongings into the beautiful, rustic farmhouse.

His family had spent the whole week packing up all of their belongings. It was a tall task! Thankfully, the McConnells were all organized people. Also, they had decided to splurge on paying for movers. That made a difference. The moving company provided the boxes, and the strong young men moved the furniture and everything else quickly and efficiently. The movers even helped pack some of the boxes on Thursday and Friday evening.

When they arrived at the new house, Martha supervised the whole unloading rigmarole alongside her husband. She was also in charge of decorating the farmhouse. The children were playing outside and had discovered an old, decrepit barn out back. As they were doing so, a tall, pallid-looking senior citizen showed up. At first, Bob was a little concerned because he didn't know who he was, but the elderly man introduced himself as Nelson, their neighbour.

After the movers unloaded all of the boxes, Martha and Bob invited Nelson in for a Coke. Thankfully, they had packed some sodas in the cooler, and their new friend was eager to accept the offer for one. Rob and Lois, the older children, joined in on the conversation from time to time, which centred on the history of the community. Nelson, an octogenarian and semiretired farmer, came from a long family line doing the same work. As the eldest son, he had inherited a large mixed farm, with both livestock and cash crops. He, his late wife and children lived off of the land, not just making a profit from selling produce and farm animals.

It turned out that a couple of Nelson's children had gone into a related business: running an abattoir not too far down the road.

"You could smell its stench from where we are right here," Nelson commented. "That is until they moved their business to Caledon."

Martha and Bob nodded their heads in agreement. They liked the idea of having a hobby farm that included animals but hadn't figured out yet to whom they would end up selling their livestock. As Bob sat back and listened to Nelson, he considered how the back-breaking work of farming had changed over the centuries. Ever since the domestication of animals in ancient times and the establishment of cities, people have tried to figure out how to ensure that food production was easier. The conversation inevitably turned in this direction.

"Y'a know the English *Enclosure Acts* were also pretty important as far as farming was concerned," Martha piped up.

Although she had no formal schooling beyond high school, she was an avid reader and knowledgeable about a variety of subjects. "Those laws guaranteed changes to previous notions of the 'commons' and allowed for the parcelling off of land that families could buy and sell freely."

Lois picked up where her mother left off. "Under the law, ownership was given to landholders, and this helped people achieve wealth that otherwise may not have been possible."

While it was true that the *Enclosure Acts* were a boon to societal development and the greater nourishment of the citizens of England, the country still had an aristocratic society at the time these laws were enacted. While these series of laws were pivotal in getting the industrial revolution going, the aristocracy still ensured that some strata of society, most notably those who owned land, would have a say in governing the nation via the House of Lords. This wasn't a bad concept, and even the United States historically didn't vote for their senators, as the thinking was that those who had a long-term ownership stake in the land would be in the best place to make significant decisions pertaining to country governance.

It was at this point that Nelson brought a moral element to the table. "You know, for all of the advancement in farming, I still think it is a challenge. As a Christian, I believe God has cursed the ground since the fall in the Garden of Eden and that by the sweat of our brow we will earn a living."

Bob chimed in about his Methodist roots and stern upbringing, but Nelson started talking about his personal relationship with his Saviour, which was an entirely new concept for Bob.

"The concept of *grace* is breathtaking," concluded Nelson. "I know I was a proverbial prodigal son in my youth…I was wayward for a time. But after I met Jesus, all of that changed. I pulled up my socks. I started taking my farming responsibilities seriously. Around that time, I met my wife, then had children. My eyes were opened to the many blessings that God chooses to bestow upon His children."

Chapter 6

It was the Victoria Day weekend. The whole McConnell family was afforded an extra day that they could use to unpack and put their special touch on the farmhouse. In preparation for a long day of hard work, they invited Nelson again, this time for a hearty breakfast of bacon, eggs and toast. The smell of coffee was percolating in the air.

"Nelson, I don't really understand what you meant when you said that we are still faced with the same curse that occurred a few thousand years ago in the time of Adam and Eve. I mean, haven't all the machine inventions coming out of the industrial revolution made farming much more efficient? Take the combine harvester, for example. It has essentially replaced the horse and the sickle." As Bob said all this, he paused for a moment from eating.

"I hear what you're saying, neighbour, but machines break down, don't they? We still experience drought!" Nelson didn't need to continue to make his point.

"I see what you mean," conceded Bob, over a sip of coffee. "I still contend, though, that farming has become substantially easier than a century ago. We're not limited to using the horse-pulled tiller, unless you're Mennonite or Amish, and modern irrigation techniques are phenomenal, along with the wonders of the internal-combustion engine. Not to mention all of the poverty that has been alleviated thanks to the agricultural revolution. So many mouths have been fed, allowing the advancement of North America, and Europe, by giving the opportunity for the industrialization process to take hold. Specialized jobs were created for workers in areas such as manufacturing. More and more people are moving to the cities or suburbs, and farming is being done by smaller and smaller percentages of the population."

Nelson smiled and poked at his food, which was already getting cold. "One thing I will say is that this fundamental law of farming still applies: You reap what you sow. A Biblical principle taken straight out of the book of Galatians. You can't fool God. If you do a bad job planting, your harvest will be less than spectacular. Garbage in, garbage out, as the saying goes."

Rob, whom no one thought was listening, added, "But once the farmer does that hard work of sowing, he has to rely on God to provide the rain." He wiped the sweat off his forehead…it was already starting to get hot, and he could smell the bacon grease, which had been absorbed by his clothes.

"Unless, of course, he is wealthy or connected enough to implement a great irrigation system." Bob remained skeptical, but he managed to get a few chuckles around the table with his comment.

***

Bob, with his boys in tow, and under the gracious direction of his new neighbour and friend, Nelson, got to work repairing some of the wooden beams of the barn. Martha and the girls unpacked the kitchen items and arranged the furniture in the living room.

As they were working away, Bob could hardly wait to venture off on his new career path of property management, and his mind wandered.

Although Bob had signed the papers for his piece of land north of Toronto, there was still one more condition of the offer that remained to be met. Bob had gotten a call from the neighbours about some sort of oil leak on the newly acquired property... Was it Carruthers? Was someone somehow envious of the new property he had acquired?

That morning, the Tuesday after Victoria Day, Bob was eager to start his business. He was in good spirits, as most of the major unpacking and some of the big fix-it jobs around the house were done already. At nine o'clock, though, he received a discouraging call from the real estate agent: there were chemicals, as well as fertilizers, from a plant a couple of miles away that had seeped into much of Bob's land.

As Bob reflected on this, he thought deeply about what Nelson meant by saying that God had put a curse on nature. Bob thought about the implications of modern technology and innovation, advancements such as the chemicals and fertilizers that had leached into the land he had almost purchased. There was a sense that good things in the world were slightly off-kilter, not as they ought to be. Why were there so many obstacles and challenges in life?

Right now Bob had to find a good lawyer who would help him sort through this mess.

***

"Yeah, this is the McConnell residence…" Bob answered, sounding a little disgruntled. It had rung multiple times, but he had just walked in the door of his home.

"My wife…she's been in an accident…" The sobs were coming on strong on the other end.

"What's the matter?"

"She was hit…in her car." By now, Bob recognized the voice amid all the emotion on the other end. It was Gord.

It all happened so suddenly. Gord's wife, Sally, was in a massive multiple-car accident along the 401, caused in part by slick roads. She was on her way home from visiting one of their children in Mississauga.

"Sally's been rushed to the Toronto General Hospital and is awaiting reconstructive surgery on both her legs. I'm about to visit her."

Bob wondered if his friend and business partner should be driving in his state of mind. But he knew he'd be doing the same thing if it were Martha who was in an accident.

All of a sudden, Bob found himself considering his own mortality. Already forty, he understood that life really was short, as all the old-timers say. He had to make the most of the time he had left.

As Bob drove down from Georgetown to visit Sally in the hospital, he tuned in to the staticky crackle of a Christian radio station. The radio host was talking about the same idea of reaping and sowing that Nelson explained not too long ago.

Bob was growing more convinced of this concept. There were certain immutable laws that governed the world. Like gravity, there was no getting around it. Both good and evil forces shaped our globe. Increasingly, Bob found himself wanting to be like the seed that fell on the good soil, as described in three of the four Gospel accounts. He didn't want to contend with the challenges of life on his own.

As Bob merged onto the highway, he thought about other Biblical stories that he admired. He always had a soft spot in his heart for the character of the Apostle Paul. What a conversion story! And that Paul lived a life on mission, though he never got married or had children. Arguably, he was the world's most effective missionary, sharing the love of Christ with many people in the years immediately following Christ's death. Joe Mittal, from Ross Henry Bruckenheimmer, was an example to Bob about what a productive life a single man could live. As a devout Christian, this former coworker was constantly volunteering and serving others, in such a selfless way.

Bob continued to think about some other Bible stories he enjoyed, including the parable of the ten minas or talents. The idea that good things have been entrusted to servants of the Lord and that a return was expected resonated with Bob. However, he was still wrestling with how this jived with grace and the prodigal son, who had royally messed up, and yet was welcomed into his father's arms without reservation or hesitation. And yet in Matthew 20, in the parable of the vineyard labourers, Jesus gives the workers the same salary, no matter when they started their work. This phenomenal notion of unmerited favour disrupted deep-seated beliefs that Bob had about the way the world operated.

Also, the concept that God's kingdom was like a hidden treasure newly discovered, a lost sheep or coin that was found again after a period of time, was beautiful. But could a just God truly accept all who came to him through the blood of Christ? Was Jesus's shed blood on the Calvary enough to atone for the sins of man, however big or small?

Maybe this struggle with doubt came about because Bob's earthly brothers were treated so well by his parents and were favoured compared to him. Bob was the only child in his family to be adopted, and he always felt that his parents adopted him out of pity. Although too young to remember, his biological parents were quite abusive. His dad was a womanizer and an alcoholic, and his mother was promiscuous. Bob's adoptive parents took him in because they figured he would be a good farmhand to have around with the seemingly endless list of chores. After all, the cows needed to be milked twice daily, the chicken and sheep needed tending to and the vegetables couldn't be neglected. From dawn to dusk, when they were not in school, all the children were expected to help their parents with the many tasks around the farm.

Chapter 7

When Bob finally arrived at the hospital, he was informed that Sally had passed away. She had fought a good fight, but the trauma of the serious collision was too much for her in the end.

There was a box of fresh Kleenexes placed beside Gord in the waiting room. Gord was even more emotional than he was over the phone a few hours ago with Bob. For a man who was generally reserved and put together, he could not stop the sobbing.

Bob remained stoic but was close to tears himself. Gord's children—a teacher in London and a sanitation engineer in Grand Bend—had not made it to the hospital yet. The hospital was sterile and had an eerily cold feel to it. The smell of antiseptic was thick in the air, and the floors were immaculately polished.

Over the next few days, as Gord and his family made the funeral arrangements, Bob decided to visit his parents in Alliston at the family farm. Perhaps he could help them with some chores. Although his parents had sold off much of the land, there was still lots to be done to keep up the property.

Once he arrived at their Alliston home, Bob called up a few attorneys he knew from his time at Ross Henry Bruckenheimmer.

They were hard-hitting lawyers who knew their stuff and would represent him well with this oil spill that had recently leaked onto his new property.

The funeral was relatively brief, a tight-knit gathering of family and friends. Gord's children and grandchildren—the whole Maxwell clan—comprised the largest segment of the attendees. The family's minister delivered the eulogy and said many thoughtful words about Sally's life. He even made an invitation for attendees to accept Christ, which Bob, without telling anyone, did in the quietness of his heart. He invited Jesus to be his leader and forgiver of sins, empowering him to live from this day forward.

Jesus's claim of being "the way, the truth, and the life," in the end, proved incontrovertible. Though the Maxwells were clearly grieving, they seemed to have an indomitable, rooted joy. A joy in eternal life. As people of faith, they lived purposefully while they were here on earth, despite the tragedies and setbacks that surely came there way.

Bob shed a tear as he reckoned the loss of his Saviour in dying at the cross for a sinful humanity. He would tell Gord later about his life-transforming decision, but not for some time. Though Bob had attended church during his childhood, he never admitted to having a true relationship with Jesus. He attended church, rather, out of a sense of obligation and duty rather than joy.

After returning back to his farmhouse in Georgetown and having already checked up on his parents in Alliston, Bob followed up with one lawyer in particular, Alfie Hourreg, from his days at Ross Henry whom he thought offered the best rate along with the best advice for the property. At this point, after his newfound faith, Bob wanted to really radiate Christ in all his interactions.

After speaking with Alfie, it was agreed that Bob's side would push the neighbours, an auto mechanic shop, to swiftly clean up the leak of oil, but would not press charges. Thankfully, it turned out that Carruthers had nothing to do with the matter. Bob was relieved.

In the meantime, Bob got his paperwork together to file for the creation of a new corporation. The latter turned out to be much easier than initially expected, as there was no backlog in such applications with the government, and the feds were actively encouraging people to start their own companies to keep the Canadian economy booming.

In the den of his farmhouse, Bob set to work researching what sort of tenants he wanted to take on in his future building, north of "the big smoke." A big, solid-oak table was covered with books from the local library—Bob brought home the limit of books and journals he was allowed to borrow. He had already spent several hours on multiple trips to the library examining periodicals, as well, which he could not bring home. Big picture ideas about the Canadian economy came to mind as Bob mulled the prospect of building a factory. Since the turn of the century, the Canadian economy had become increasingly industrialized. He wanted to stay ahead of the curve and, obviously, create a prosperous business.

Factories were springing up in the major metropolitan areas. Where once agriculture was the staple of the Canadian economy, companies that produced durable goods were becoming the mainstay of the economy. More and more machine automation meant that industries that had thrived in previous eras, such as the handcrafting of furniture, were becoming rare.

In all of his thinking and planning, Bob knew he had to involve his business partner, Gord. While doing his research, Bob took thorough, copious notes to present a case to Gord about how they should construct the building and what type of tenants they would want take on.

***

"I'm broke, Bob."

Silence.

"I discovered this when I was looking through our latest financial statements." Gord continued, looking sheepishly at the floor and not sure what to expect next.

"Well, whadda we do about it?" Gord was fazed. His mind was elsewhere; he was too distracted by his wife's recent passing.

"I have enough to get us through a few weeks…" Bob didn't need to ask any more questions. He knew the death of God's wife hit him hard financially, judging from a few conversations he had had lately with his business partner. "In a few months, though, we'll have to go fishing for some more money!"

Chapter 8

The documentary Bob was watching droned on. He had already studied Marshall McLuhan, and knew the significance of the development of the television set. Bob wondered why he was even bothering watching this seemingly low-budget show. For better or worse, many North American families were buying TVs. It was replacing the radio as the choice form of entertainment. Some people thought they were wonderful, but the older Bob got, the more he saw them as a time-waster and filling his children's brains with useless information.

In Bob's eyes, *Hockey Night in Canada* was an acceptable program, though. Even before the television came around, families would gather around the radio for the weekly game. *The Friendly Giant* was another innocent TV show, but many others were downright silly and did not inspire the populace to think deeply or critically. Although Bob watched the news on TV, he saw no reason why people shouldn't be literate enough to pick up the newspaper and read to find out what was going on in the world.

As Bob put the finishing touches on his package to file for incorporation, he watched his children in front of the television.

They were so innocent at their ages! He had big dreams for his children and wanted to teach them as much as he could before they left his home.

The same lawyer that helped him manage the situation pertaining to the leaked chemicals on the business property assisted Bob in putting together the articles of incorporation and the application form for the Department of National Revenue.

"McConnell Maxwell Developments Limited" was the uncreative name that Bob and Gord had settled on for their nascent corporation. The company would develop the land in question, then find at least one tenant to occupy the building. As agreed on with his wife, Bob would continue to broker second mortgages and be a landlord for residential tenants on the side. Gord would also do some repair of heavy machinery to supplement his income. Bob was even trying to figure out how he might ask Nelson to give them a hand in their new endeavour.

Bob got up to go to the study he had created on the second floor of his farmhouse. Upon entering the room, he noticed that he had just received a telex from a friend of his who was a successful real estate developer. The telex listed a number of reputable construction firms that built towers and other facilities for the commercial real estate market. After the Second World War, the number of such firms had skyrocketed. The general population was booming, optimism was in the air and it seemed as if buildings were springing up everywhere.

Gord and Bob shook hands with Tom Higgs near the entrance to the bank. Considering it was only June, the weather was sweltering.

All three men walked to the rear of the building and went inside of a crowded cubicle brimming with paper. Higgs closed the door behind him. Gord and Bob were hard up for cash as they had exhausted all of their immediate reserves to get their business off the ground.

"So you want a loan, do you?" Higgs asked, as he lit a pipe.

"You bet," said Bob, assuredly.

"And you're an established company?"

"Not established," admitted Gord. "We're starting out. We plan on developing a prime piece of real estate in the north end of Toronto."

"I'm with you…but we need some guarantee if you folks go belly up."

Bob was prepared with an answer. He had discussed the matter already with his colleague. "Well, we both own houses, paid off in full."

Higgs still looked hesitant. "That's good but not good enough. You're asking for five hundred thousand dollars to build a factory, and that's all you got for collateral?"

At this point, the two business partners were a little unprepared and thinking on their feet.

"I've got a business of brokering second mortgages on the side…I'm a successful landlord. I had money in investments and savings, but the costs for tenant repairs and for a lawyer has been astronomical. Not to mention that my wife and I recently acquired a farm, which we hope to allow us to supplement our income."

Higgs gave both men a long, hard stare. "I see…well, I can authorize a loan for four hundred and fifty thousand dollars and not a penny more," stated the banker authoritatively, doing some quick calculations and billowing ringlets of smoke in the air. "Fill out the paperwork here, and return it to my secretary when you leave."

***

McConnell Maxwell Developments was overjoyed to secure financing for their building. Though it wasn't fully what they had costed out, it would do. Bob had made sure to go in with a high figure so that he could get the money for which he had hoped.

The contractor they had chosen for constructing the building was a client of a client that Gord knew. This contractor was offering the best price and value for their dollar and, as a local company, knew how to source the project without overspending on materials and going in the red. The clincher was the architectural blueprints. Bob's older brother, Warren, was to submit a first draft of them next week. To reimburse him, Bob had been able to get his brother to agree to barter: in exchange for Warren's services, Bob would provide some fresh produce next season from the family farm.

All told, the project was moving ahead with relative ease. "If you can't do a job the proper way, don't do it at all," Bob's father would tell his children. McMax Developments, for short, was doing all it could to have a quality building built while all the while being mindful of the cost.

With the positive headway being made by McMax Developments and financing secured, Bob felt he should treat himself to a hunting trip in Quebec. Though he wasn't yet able to return to Nunavut, Northwest Territories or Yukon, he was happy to achieve a level of serenity in the wilderness for a short while. Northern Canada was rife with all sorts of game: moose, deer, pheasant, the list went on.

It was October, and Bob had solicited the services of the outfitter Boucher & fils to help him in his quest to hunt deer. Bob and his guide, Guy, flew up to a remote corner of the Laurentides in a de Havilland Otter plane. Unexperienced in flying on such small aircraft, Bob clutched his armrests for dear life as the aircraft was tossed and turned in massive gales.

It didn't make matters any better that Guy's grasp of English was rather shaky. A Métis originally from Tadoussac, Guy used to lead groups of tourists on whale-watching expeditions. What mattered, though, was that Guy was warm-hearted and friendly. In the end, Bob was able to hunt a deer in just an hour! For Guy, this was a record. After preparing the meat to bring home, Bob made mental notes of all the occasions and people with whom he would share the treat.

First, though, the venison had to be smoked. It took longer to smoke the meat—about two and a half hours—than it did to actually catch the deer. They also made sausages and neatly packaged them. Bob intended to use them as gifts for people he knew and who were special to him. Since the deer was large, there was plenty of meat to go around to people who were dear to his heart. On the plane ride back to Ontario, Bob dozed off and dreamt of returning to Quebec's Eastern Townships, going to a sugar shack and skiing on Mont Orford…with his whole family.

Bob fastidiously looked over the blueprints for his new building. The devil was in the details. Although he initially thought that the prints were A-okay, Patterson Construction Ltd., the building contractor, had returned them to him because they weren't specific enough.

Although Warren was a bright guy, he had only taken a couple of courses in architecture. Bob started to understand this when he was reading some of the builder's comments on the proposed design, asking for further clarification. Warren hadn't prepared blueprints himself in a while, not since he had moved up the chain of command at the home builder over the last twenty years, and his licence was due to expire very soon.

***

Bob passed along the blueprints back to his brother. Warren apologized for the confusion and had one of his associates rectify the errors. This time, Bob shelled out some company coin to cover the cost of fixing the errors, although he still promised to give some fresh fruits and vegetables to Warren during next year's crop season.

With the coming of winter, Bob had to do work around the farm. In the fall, the McConnell family had bought a few chickens, some cows and a couple of horses. Bob needed to ensure that the barn would be suitable for the animals during the cold, snowy months. Some of the fences badly needed mending, too.

This will all be fine, Bob thought to himself. During those times over the winter when he had work to do at the farmhouse, he would not be bogged down with the new building development as construction couldn't begin when the ground was frozen. Then, come spring, construction on the business property would be in full swing.

The farmhouse was a cozy place to be in the winter. There was a large wood-burning stove that was centrally located in the home, giving it a glowing warmth. When the home was built in 1842, oil lamps would have been used to read and enjoy games in the evening. Today, electricity powered much of the home's lighting needs at nighttime. Bob was glad he didn't have to worry about oil lamps and the danger they posed to causing fires at the home.

Chapter 9

Now that the blueprints were fully fixed and ready to be used, construction was about to begin. Easter had come and gone, spring was in the air and the ground had already thawed. Patterson Construction Ltd. was raring to go, dispatching their men to start digging the foundation for the building that was to appear at Yonge and Steeles. Bob and Gord had decided that the building would contain a factory with two tenants.

At seven-thirty on the Monday morning after the Easter weekend, about a week after the construction had begun, all five workmen had arrived on site early. The idea was that if they came in early, they could leave early, and this would be especially good once the weather turned scorching during the summer months. However, on this day, with work having barely begun, a tragedy occurred. Rex, one of the younger recruits on the team, had wandered too close to the hole that the backhoes were digging.

"Watch out, Rex!" yelled Bud as he saw his friend back up near the hole for the foundation. Bud was desperately trying to get the young construction worker's attention.

"*Hhheeeeellllppp!!!!*" The blood curdling cry came out loud and clear.

It was too late.

Rex fell backward into the hole and was knocked unconscious, and work had to cease immediately while the paramedics were called, and first aid was administered.

A swarm of construction workers flocked to Rex's side in a heartbeat. Everyone was prepared for accidents, but were caught off guard by what just happened.

The paramedics had to very carefully extricate Rex from the foundation hole that was partially dug and rush him to the hospital. While the man would end up living, he was in critical condition, and he needed to be connected to oxygen and a plethora of other tubes. His family immediately joined him at his hospital bedside. His wife was so thankful that they lived in Canada and could take advantage of universal healthcare.

Despite the setback, once Rex was removed from the scene and given medical attention, the four remaining workers continued. The foundation was nearly all dug out. Now, the steel girders needed to be put in place. Cranes were brought in to do this task. After, the building structure would be filled in using poured concrete and cinder blocks for the small office located in the front of the building. In total, the building would be three stories high.

Bob worked several hours that evening getting the animals out of the barn and cleaning out the stalls. His children assisted him in bringing out the horses and cows to the field, as well as allowing the chickens to move to their springtime coup that was slightly outside of the barn. The barn had once been a coach house where horse-and-buggy would stay overnight. It was magnificently built. Bob also had to put some netting up and fill holes up where the groundhogs had recently wreaked havoc. The next time he saw one of these pests he would use his handy rifle he had hanging on the wall.

Upon retreating to the house, Bob stopped in to give his wife a peck on the cheek. She was busy knitting away for her children, which along with general clothing repair and baking had kept her quite occupied over the winter. Bob had helped with much of the canning and preserving of fruit. He had set aside a few cans and venison sausage for his brother, Warren, who had helped with the blueprints for Bob's commercial property.

Bob had always been a fan of history. Now that he was living in the countryside, he took a particular interest in his family ancestral tree. In his research, and through visiting various local museums, he had learned that many of his family members were United Empire Loyalists. This meant that after the War of 1812, those relatives had moved to Canada to live. They were loyal to the reigning monarch of Great Britain.

"Martha, did you know that the British monarchy, in its heyday of the nineteenth century, was extraordinarily impressive. It was said that the sun never set on the empire. Indeed, the positive effects of this benevolent empire are still being felt. The English language was the language of business, and countries in the Commonwealth, such as Australia, Canada, New Zealand and South Africa, have enjoyed high standards of living for decades. What's more, other countries such as India in recent years have experienced explosive growth. Some may say that this was the result of independence from the English, but the English legal system had pervaded the country, getting it on track for economic development."

Unfazed, Martha responded, "You're right, and the development of other countries, such as China, have been increasing at a fast rate. Teachings from Marx and Engels have turned that particular society into an official Communist one. I still think, though, the best form of government to have existed is the one that gives power to the people—a democracy. Sure, populism was attractive, but not enduring like the democracies of Western Europe, England, the United States and Canada. For a government to be effective at governing, there needed to be checks and balances to power, which should be present in democratic institutions."

Kathy, who had entered the room, piped up, "Know what? Since the Second World War, the West had really come together in solidarity, under the banner of NATO. The countries subject to the Warsaw Pact needed to be kept in line, and NATO was the most efficient way to do so. The doctrine of d-e-t-err-ence," she said, sounding out the syllable to herself, "or mutually assured destruction… meant that the United States, in the Cold War, wanted to arm themselves with sufficient nuclear capability to wipe out the enemy should an attack occur. It's my grade eleven history teacher who taught me this!"

Bob interjected, "Despite time passing, such as the investigations during the 1950's put together by Senator Joseph McCarthy in the United States, democracy did have much to offer citizens of Russia. In democracies, we take capital markets and efficient distribution of goods for granted. Central planning had failed to ensure that the peasant class achieved adequate food to survive and thrive. The series of five-year plans did not prove to be the golden ticket for resolving the Soviet Union's problems.

"In the meritocracies of the West, so long as you worked hard, you could earn a living to provide for your family. Only in extreme cases such as world wars did rationing of milk, butter and sugar occur; otherwise, goods were reasonably equitably distributed to those who worked for them. No doubt, there was poverty. Inner cities weren't above ghettoization. But on the whole, citizens could rise to their full potential and earn their keep in Western countries."

Martha got up for cold apple juice but added her opinion. "The problem of poverty, in Judeo-Christian countries, was thought to be under the purview of the church and the community. Communist countries, on the other hand, relied on government intervention to redistribute wealth. Although Soviet society had developed lots of nuclear weapons, it lacked a spiritual component that was evident in the hopelessness that its citizenry felt. What's more, the regulation and interference of government meant that many citizens could not get basic products in stores due to shortages, harkening back to a feudal Europe comprised of serfs and landless peasants."

Everyone enjoyed cool drinks as they further discussed politics and international relations—a new family pastime.

***

The Toronto property was in its final stages of being built. Bob had to cough up more money from his personal investments, and Gord had to refinance his home to pay for the rest of the project.

After having inspected the progress, which included the painted walls and installation of the heating, ventilation and air conditioning systems, Bob travelled back to his home. He put the finishing touches on the fence he was mending around his family property. It was a project he had been meaning to complete for a while now.

His children did what they could in aiding their father with the job. Paul passed him the tools, and Rob transported the wood in a wheelbarrow to repair and remove the broken pieces along the fence. Before long, the job was finished. Then, Bob and Rob chopped wood for their stove, carefully putting it in the shed to allow it to dry.

Chapter 10

There were so many passages in the Bible that compared the similarity of building a good building and building one's life on the solid rock of Christ. Like Bob's new building, if he only learned to trust Jesus in all aspects of his life, Bob would be certain that he was following Christ's will.

The whole McConnell clan had been attending weekly services for a year now. The subject of the talk the minister was preaching on this past Sunday at the local Presbyterian church was the seventh chapter of Matthew's gospel, which taught us that if we built our foundation on Jesus Christ, we would have a solid foundation in times of trouble. Again, in Ephesians 2:19–20, we saw how we, as Christians, "built on the foundations of the apostles and prophets, with Christ Jesus as our chief cornerstone."

The minister joked that Bob should preach next Sunday and talk about his practical experience constructing an office building and how doing so required careful thought and consideration, just like when we build our spiritual lives in Christ. Bob laughed but agreed that he'd be open to preaching in the near future.

***

Sunday afternoon, back on the farm, Bob was working again. Nelson had joined him. It was a 24/7 job, and the McConnell family were experiencing how much work it really was, especially after having been given three pigs and five sheep. How were they going to manage with all these farm animals? Bob was thankful that his Heavenly Father was a far better shepherd than he'd ever be!

This year they were growing corn, and Bob was seeding the corn with the farm equipment Nelson had leant him. In exchange, he would receive some of the harvest. Bob also had to figure out how to rotate the crops so that the farm could be sustainable. The question of sustainability—making a livelihood off the land—was similar to the questions with which developing nations had to grapple. Thankfully, the Dominion of Canada's rule of law had held firm, and hard-working farmers often prospered, if they were willing to learn and employ the latest techniques common to other people in their field. The dirty thirties was the exception, but much wisdom had been gleaned from that era, and Bob hoped a Depresssion like that would not repeat itself.

The world powers such as Portugal, Spain, England, Holland and France had colonized Africa and South America. With the escalation of the Cold War, decolonization led to the demise of these powers and left a vacuum in the former colonies. The prevailing thought was that these newly independent states ought to modernize, chiefly through technological development and agricultural reform. Nevertheless, the presence of civil wars in these regions meant that competing factions in power had stopped many of these countries from moving forward and improving their gross national products.

The north Toronto factory building was complete. The builders passed along the keys to Bob. Hard to believe all of this was completed already! Now, it was just a question of getting good tenants. Bob had already placed advertisements in *The Globe and Mail* as well as in *The Star*. The response was overwhelming. So many companies were interested in leasing!

After picking up the keys for the building, Bob stopped by Gord's place with his list of prospective tenants. On this particular day, Lois, Bob's second eldest, had a date with a boy from the high school football team. This distracted him on the drive down because he objected on two counts: Lois was too young to be going out, and it was a weeknight to boot! He would not allow this to happen again.

***

Upon meeting up with Gord, the list of prospective tenants was whittled down to two. One was a shoe factory, and the other was a textile mill. Each business partner would be responsible for preparing one of the leases. Since Bob had experience preparing leases from renting rooms in his previous house in Toronto, he gave some tips to Gord over coffee about how to draft up his business lease.

During the drive back to Georgetown, Bob turned his mind to other matters. He tried to figure out how he would get his cows to reproduce. He had decided that he didn't want to have a bull because they were too dangerous. Bob wanted to send some of the cows to Nelson's children's abattoir down the road from the farmhouse and make some money on the side. The idea of using artificial insemination was a possibility. This modern option would likely be the route that Bob would take.

Juggling his company affairs and farming responsibility was a big load. Bob's father, Edward, had taught him this strong work ethic. Bob, as an adopted child from a large orphanage just outside of Orillia, had been expected to pull his weight on the farm. In those days, social services were not taken on by the government. Instead, orphanages cared for babies that resulted from unwed mothers or unexpected pregnancies. What's more, the foster care system did not really exist. Young orphans did not go from home to home to home. Instead, they were matched with a family. Some families were good to those orphans, others not so good.

The family Bob grew up in certainly had its share of issues, though. Alcohol and adultery were persistent problems. But as a new believer in Christ, Bob was strengthened by his relationship with Jesus. The Lord, himself, promised to his followers that he would not leave them as orphans. As a result, Christians were commanded to look after widows and orphans in their distress, as the book of James explained. This was a task that Bob wanted to commit himself to carry out in the future.

Chapter 11

With both tenant leases signed, Gord and Bob showed the two company CEOs the new facilities. The building was mostly empty, and both employers were going to split, roughly fifty-fifty, the two-hundred-thousand-square-foot location. There was also a large loading dock out back, as well as a sizable parking lot.

The CEOs were very well-dressed. One had cufflinks with a pinstriped shirt, and the other had a fancy bow tie and a starched, crisp white shirt. Both men obviously paid close attention to the image they conveyed with their dress. Bob wondered what the executive pay was now. It had really taken off in recent years. Now, mind you, both these companies were around fifty years old, so they had sufficient time to grow and establish themselves in the market and with their shareholders.

But the disparity in pay between CEOs and workers was becoming several multiples of the pay of the average worker. Bob was no communist, yet he recognized the rights of workers to decent wages that rewarded the workers. It was the fight for pay equity, along with employees' desire to improve working conditions, that led to the rise of unions, Bob reckoned. This started in the nineteenth century and gained traction by the current century. Even the public sector was becoming unionized! The trade guilds of past eras were quickly being replaced by the collectivization of the union movement. The culmination, of course, centring on union activity occurred during the Winnipeg General Strike of 1919. The RCMP needed to be called in to enforce order as the whole affair quickly got out of hand.

At the present time, Bob was glad that he was in business for himself. The deals that he had just struck up between Jones Shoes and Marvin Textiles seemed like a match made in heaven. The textile mill even provided material to the shoemakers. It was a deal from which both companies benefited.

Bob had just celebrated his forty-first birthday. Hard to believe how time was flying. He was growing more concerned that Lois was up to no good with that football captain boyfriend of hers. Bob thought that her boyfriend wasn't the right fit for her, although he was happy that she was starting to date. Even Kathy was curious about boys at the tender age of fourteen. Bob was glad that Paul had years before he would start dating, let alone leave home. Rob, on the other hand, at seventeen years old was so serious in his relationship with his girlfriend, Joy, that Bob wouldn't be surprised if he proposed to her sooner or later.

The emerging hippy generation believed in free love and world peace. They were trying to throw off the shackles of the *Leave It to Beaver* generation of their parents. Bob knew enough from what he read of the Bible that world peace would not come until the millennial kingdom! The younger people of the 1960s were being promiscuous, shirking marriage and other institutions in society that were once considered basic.

Gosh, thought Bob, everyone knew that romantic love was temporary. What lasted was *commitment*. When a man married a woman, he committed himself to her. Through sickness and health, for richer or poorer, whatever the circumstance the two would face, they would do so together. Common-law relationships did not produce the covenantal relationship that God intended between men and women.

Whoever would be great must become least...To him who is faithful more will be given...Whoever is great among you must be servant of all...It is difficult for a rich man to enter heaven. The teachings of Jesus were staggering. Truthfully, Bob wanted to be prosperous and wealthy—financially independent. But he saw how this would become an idol, unless he sacrificed it at his Saviour's feet.

To keep himself humble, Bob volunteered weekly at a drop-in centre in downtown Georgetown. Man, these people have it rough, he thought. Many of them were caught in a string of bad decisions or had experienced difficult childhoods. Drugs, addictions and lives held in bondages by the enemy kept these men and women from achieving the potential that God had in mind for them when he created them.

The minister of Bob's church, Ralph, ran the weekly outreach and always presented the attendees with a simple Gospel message at the end, after a time of pickup basketball and some card playing or board games. Ralph would ask if anyone wanted to accept Jesus as their Lord and Saviour. A handful of people would raise their hands, with everyone's eyes closed. Some keyboardist would be playing the sweet melody of a praise song in the background. It was in that moment that Bob realized what he was made for…and it wasn't for making cash. He was made to "live a life worthy of the calling" as it said in Ephesians. He was meant to walk with his Lord daily.

Back on the farm, the sap that Bob, with the help of Nelson, had tapped this year had been plentiful. Strong, tall sugar maple trees lined the fence along Bob's property, both in front and to the side. Bob was strongly considering buying additional property near his farmhouse. To the east was Nelson's farmstead, to the south was the gravel road and to the west and north Bob was in negotiations to buy it from the two families that owned those tracks of land.

If he was successful in acquiring the new land, Bob could practise crop rotation on a larger scale: one hundred acres could be for sheep and cows to graze, one hundred acres could be for a crop of some sort and then the other one hundred acres could go fallow for a year. The practice of letting fields lay fallow dated back to Biblical times. In addition, the year of Jubilee was a remarkable celebration when the various debts that folks had accumulated would be pardoned, and people were free to start again with a blank financial slate. Bob also liked the ideas of leaving grain for the poor to glean and being kind to the newcomer in the land. He was trying to implement as much of these ideas as possible in his own farm.

Chapter 12

After the successful birth of the new calf and a bumper crop, word of Bob's farming abilities started to spread across Georgetown. Now, instead of his family selling produce at the side of the road, which Kathy had taken on while she was supervising her younger brother, Paul, the McConnells were starting to bring in their produce to the weekly farmers' market.

The farmers' market had mixed results. What was sold was for the most part dictated by the weather. When the weather was pleasant—warm but not overly hot or sticky—the produce sold like hotcakes. If it were overcast or rainy, the fruits and vegetables were slow to sell. The market ran from May to October every year. The family was even bringing in cherries from the trees that were sprinkled around their house, as well as pears. The challenge with the cherries, though, was that they needed to be doused in pesticides so the bugs wouldn't get to them.

Bob's real estate business was becoming more profitable. Special provisions in the lease allowed Gord and Bob to capitalize on the profits of the companies who were renting the factory space. Even still, there were unexpected expenses, as well as the usual wear and tear of the property. Bob hired a company to install carpets in the front office and even a window air conditioner. The idea of trying to sell the company became increasingly appealing.

But with the increase in wealth came the unique temptations that riches had to bring. The Lord taught his followers not to store away treasures in barns where they would rot. Instead, we were to faithfully serve him. Luke 17 highlighted how we were not even to expect a *thank you* but that our attitude with regard to serving our Heavenly Father was to come from a place knowing that we were unworthy of the gifts bestowed upon us.

The extreme wealth in Canada was concentrated in the hands of a few wealthy families. For instance, Roy Thomson had become a very successful businessman with diversified acquisitions and holdings. Bob knew that if he ever became very wealthy, he wanted to give away a lot of his money to philanthropic and Christian causes. In the end, he and his business partner ended up selling the company.

With the company sold, Bob had hundreds of thousands of dollars sitting in the bank. Life was good. Gord used the money from the sale to sock away for his young grandchildren's education. Bob was desperately trying to not let the positive circumstances get to his head. But he found himself reading books like *Six Easy Steps to Getting Rich Fast*, *14 Habits of the Wealthy* and *No-Brainer Ways to Get Cash Quickly*.

Martha warned him that these sorts of books were not helpful to read. He was going to be make wealth an idol, if he had not already done so. She said that his money was going to his head.

With the investment that Bob had made in real estate, over the wintertime, he was ready to move on to his next business venture. He had agreed to join a consulting firm, and then ended up freelancing shortly thereafter. Over the last few years, the whole industry had been growing rapidly. With the specialization of firms came the increase in professional advice-giving, on any number of topics.

The niche that Bob was hoping to develop was agricultural consulting. Although Bob had never been a serious farmer, he knew he was good enough at it to make a living.

In some ways, his new work foray reminded him of his first career, working at Ross Henry Bruckenheimmer. It had the same intensity to it. But Bob had greater flexibility: he was often able to work from home and got to travel extensively to meet with clients. In fact, Bob usually only went to WorldConsult Canada, the Guelph-based consultancy company he worked for, a handful of times per week. He tried to, obviously, pick and choose which days were best for him depending on his family's schedule and when traffic would be best.

Bob even took apart his Massey Ferguson tractor and put it back together again, with Gord's help. The tractor itself wasn't broken, but Bob was honing his skills. He wanted to familiarize himself with farming equipment as much as possible. The contract that he was working on was with a consortium of farmers who pooled their resources for the betterment of their farms.

Having been back and forth a few times from Saskatchewan, Bob had learned a great deal about the province. Tommy Douglas, the famed leader of the social democratic party, whom he had met by chance at the airport, was a legend there. As the premier of Saskatchewan, he told Bob about how he ensured that his province was the first in the country to adopt universal medicare. Bob was fortunate to get his signature on book he had brought on his trip.

What's more, Douglas had a deep understanding of his faith. He acted on what he preached. The thinking was, that as Christians, we needed to live out a life of faith that embraced social justice and the commitment to a more equitable society, fair toward all people.

Truly, the poor in society needed our help. They were not always the victim of circumstance. The Good News of Jesus needed to be lived out for all to see so that some people could come to faith in him. For this reason, Bob volunteered regularly with the orphanage that he was started near Orillia. Gord, a Christian himself, volunteered alongside Bob. Although it was a couple hours' drive from Georgetown, they stayed with relatives overnight during the times they volunteered there. Together, they put a fresh coat of paint on the walls of the facility. Bob even considered being foster parents, but needed to thoroughly discuss the matters with his wife first.

Chapter 13

On a bone-chilling February night, Bob was playing euchre with his family. The older he got, the more he loved spending quality time with his loved ones. Not everyone was blessed with the gift of children, but Bob wanted to make the most of this gift with his family. For the time being, though, Bob and his wife thought they would not have foster children due to the busyness of moving and the demands of his career.

His eldest boy was already engaged. He was on the right path in life. Having made a personal commitment in his faith, he was determined to follow Jesus in his decision making. Although Rob had considered working in the trades, in the end, he ended up signing up for the Royal Canadian Air Force. He knew that it would be the key to getting his education paid in full as a mechanical engineer. Rob wanted to build things. But first he desired to serve in the Canadian military. This whole opportunity was aided greatly by Rob's years of training as an air cadet.

The truth was that Canada, though, did not intervene in many international skirmishes. Sure, we were involved in the First and Second World Wars, as well as the Korean War, but aside from those conflicts, Canada tended to stick to peacekeeping. It was what earned Lester B. Pearson the Nobel Peace Prize in 1956 during the Suez crisis.

Canada was constantly trying to exert its soft power, especially when it came to our relationship with our neighbours to the south. We felt that we could be that prudent voice urging caution or showing the Americans a better way.

But during the Cold War, a lot was painted in black and white. If you were on the American side, you were against Communism. If you were on the Soviet side, the Americans were the bad guys. The Cuban Missile Crisis nearly brought the world to the brink of nuclear war. But, thank the Lord, civilization persisted.

Despite the new job, Bob was getting bored. He was used to spending more time around the farm and less time jetting around from place to place and meeting in boardrooms. Also, as much as he enjoyed farming, he preferred doing it as a hobby. He didn't want to involve himself, even in a consulting capacity, in farming on a full-time basis.

Nevertheless, he plugged away at his job, and client led to client, referral to referral. He even did work with the Canadian Wheat Board and the newly formed Dairy Commission. Clearly, there was a move toward more solidarity in the agricultural community, for the benefit of all farmers. But did that have a communist bent to it? Was the West more socialist than the rest of Canada?

Probably not. There were plenty of rednecks in Alberta and business-minded individuals in British Columbia, thought Bob. Compared to the United States, though, Canada tended to be a little more left-leaning.

Yet, in the Prairies, it made sense to organize in collectives and look out for one's neighbour, so to speak. The dust bowl and the economic hardship of the 1930s meant that the reality of farming was best carried out when everyone's mutual interest was shared. Even the tough homesteaders of the late-nineteenth and early twentieth centuries would be glad to have a community of support, where fair prices for grain and wheat could be established for the good of all.

So Bob was looking for his next career move. He still wasn't ready to retire yet, but he was seeking deeper fulfillment from a different career.

Then the call came. Bob was relaxing on one of his days off from work when he got a call that would change the rest of his career.

"So you're looking for a career change?" the caller said.

"How did you know?" Bob felt that the caller, who had yet to identify himself, was reading his mind.

The caller took that as a yes. "I think you'll like the oil industry."

Bob had had enough. He wasn't opposed to a career change, but he wanted to know who was on the other line.

"I may be interested…but who's this, may I ask?"

The caller paused. It was Jack Johnston, the chairman of the board of CanGas Inc. A wealthy and powerful rancher from Barons, Alberta. Rumour had it he wore a cowboy hat to board meetings.

Bob didn't need time to think. He immediately agreed to the job offer of chief executive officer. What Bob was really curious about was how Mr. Johnston obtained his contact information. Was he referred to him via a head hunting agency? Did a friend recommend Bob to CanGas?

Either way, Bob saw this as an opportunity to seize—a chance to jump into yet a third career in only a couple of short years.

Chapter 14

The culture of CanGas was one that was highly organized. It was a company much like Standard Oil, the enormous financial empire amassed by John D. Rockefeller. The unfettered capitalism that had been rampant in the United States never really caught on in Canada.

Canada had its geniuses, Bob reckoned, like Nova Scotian Alexander Graham Bell, who invented the telephone, although it was still disputed: was he American, Scottish or Canadian? Another good example of Canadian genius was Frederick Banting, who invented insulin. But his sidekick, Charles Best, from Maine, worked alongside Banting in discovering the famed medicine for diabetes.

Yet even the American steel titan Andrew Carnegie was born in Scotland. It showed that many North American heroes were immigrants. As for the person who invented the zipper, many thought he was Canadian, but again he was someone who lived in Canada and was of Swedish extraction; he also spent time in the United States. Clearly, the world was a global village!

Bombardier, though, was a good example of a successful Canadian company. However, part of its success was because it not only developed great products that were useful and that people wanted to buy but it was a tightly knit, family-controlled business that resisted pressures from the outside.

This philosophy was similar to the operating principles at CanGas, Bob considered, as he scrawled in his daily journal. The management, aside from Bob, verged on the autocratic. Bob was happy that Gord had taken an early retirement. He would be able to enjoy himself at home, tinker with his toys and not have to face the big decisions that Bob would now be facing, in the limelight and under the scrutiny of knowledgeable investors.

As Bob penned the date, he was suddenly overwhelmed with how quickly time passed. It was 1963, and Lester B. Pearson had just launched the Commission on Bilingualism and Biculturalism. Would Canada get its own distinct flag? Perhaps it was time to truly cut the apron strings from Great Britain, and change our national flag from the ensign. Bob was also concerned that government was concerned was the encroachment on society. It seemed as if more and more public service jobs were being created, industries were being increasingly regulated and social services were multiplying greatly. Bob tried to capture all this in his journal. What was next? Was the government going to somehow guarantee jobs for its citizenry?

It felt like a whiff of socialism, but these thoughts were far from Bob's mind as he sat in the boardroom on Bay Street, not too far from the location of his old investment firm. Bob promptly put away his journal as the meeting started.

The chairman of the board, Jack Johnston, started talking and gave a few introductory remarks. A stalwart figure hailing from the prestigious Leaside neighbourhood, with an education from Upper Canada College and a background in law from Osgoode Hall Law School at the University of Toronto.

Jack acknowledged the work of Bob's predecessor, Sid Kanastasis, a hard-working gentleman who was forced into retirement earlier in the spring, after having spent nearly twenty years at the helm of the company, and his entire career at the firm.

"I'd like to thank you all for your hard work and dedication over the last few months. I would also like to welcome our new chief executive, Robert Timothy McConnell, to the company. His diverse and skilled background will truly be an asset to this organization, and I expect your full support during his time here."

A young female clerk distributed photostats of an agenda and a handout with facts and figures.

Next, the CFO spoke. It seemed like there was a consensus around the room that CanGas actually wanted to diversify its portfolio aggressively. The CFO, Mike Mandriki, mentioned how the company was hoping to take advantage of all the mining opportunities accessible to Canadians.

"In addition to our exploratory Athabasca oil sands ventures, we would like to broaden the expanse of our company…we see great opportunity in the mineral deposits in Canada's North," Mandriki said, with a shimmer in his eye.

As Bob sat on the plane, returning back home, ethical questions abounded as he considered the issues facing him as CEO. He had to grow the company without taking advantage of anyone in the corporation. In the context of CanGas, Bob had to ensure that Indian groups were being treated fairly and were being negotiated with in good faith.

Bob had to travel up to Yellowknife to scout out some keen business opportunities. The Mackenzie Valley was such a promising place to work. In addition to having acquired three small, local companies this past year alone from the Northwest Territories and Yukon, CanGas wanted to open up some of their own mines. This involved close cooperation with the federal government and the two territorial governments.

Bob flew in a Cessna aircraft in areas of the Canadian wilderness that were near the treeline. The beauty was incredible. Where there were trees, they were evergreens. The winters were far too harsh in this part of the country for deciduous trees to survive.

When Bob arrived back in Calgary, at the regional headquarters, he had to figure out how the company would finance the expansion of their business. As Bob had mentioned to an interviewer on the CBC radio a few days ago, the company was planning on raising money in a very traditional way: selling more shares of the company.

The corporate strategy being employed was a clever one. CanGas executives would retain control of the decision making by keeping preferred, Class A shares. Meanwhile, additional shares would be issued to stockholders in the form of Class B, nonvoting shares. This would be great debt financing, which the company would pay back to Canadian shareholders as it enjoyed greater profits resulting from prosperous mineral operations across the country.

CanGas was pursuing prospects in South America too. Venezuela, Argentina and Colombia held vast amounts of natural resources, similar to Canada. The company engaged in a couple of hostile takeovers through the acquisition of a gold mine and an oil company.

But Bob had major problems with these corporate actions. They were undertaken well before he assumed his responsibilities as CEO and occurred in an authoritarian regime.

Chapter 15

CanGas was building its brand, and Bob was at the centre of it. It was already looking forward to its role in the 1967 Canadian centennial celebrations. With centennial celebrations less than three years away, CanGas was already organizing the booth that it was going to have at Expo 67 in Montreal, Quebec. Bob had the responsibility of making sure this went swimmingly...

This was all part of the strong corporate image that the company was trying to develop. CanGas felt that Western Canada, with its abundance of oil sands and other natural resources, like potash, was going to be the great economic engine to drive Canada. But other people, including Bob, wondered about how the volatility of commodity markets would play out on the Canadian markets in downtimes. In order to not be pulled down by low commodity prices, Canada needed to have a diverse economy comprising the perfect combination of advanced manufacturing, agriculture and natural resource development sectors.

Bob—tasked with preparing a memorandum on use of computers at CanGas—had heard about the International Business Machines (IBM) company and its tremendous corporate growth.

Currently, these machines were the size of a room. But the capabilities appeared to be limitless! Take farming, for instance: what if cows could be milked via machines in a large-scale environment? The profitability of such an endeavour would be formidable.

***

Bob McConnell finished his iced tea on a dog day of summer after a long day of chores on the farm. He got ready for bed, said goodnight to his children and gave his wife a peck on the cheek before settling in to bed.

After having turned off the light, he pulled the sheets over himself and turned toward the wall. The next thing he knew, he felt the cold, steely barrel of a gun pointed at him, on his forehead. A trickle of sweat formed down his back. It was life or death, fight-or-flight.

Before he knew it, his mouth was gagged, and he was knocked unconscious and dragged out of his house. By the time Bob regained consciousness, he realized he was travelling down the road at breakneck speed in the back of a van, with a pillowcase over his head. The road felt bumpy, and Bob felt utterly out of control of his surroundings.

He could hear some shouting back and forth. He guessed it was Spanish, although he could not be certain given his limited grasp of the language.

Finally, the van came to an abrupt stop.

Chapter 16

When the dust settled and Bob figured out where he was, it was quite the scene. Big, burly men were sitting around him smoking pipes and cigars. Bob's hands were handcuffed to the chair he was sitting in.

In front of him, Bob could see a steel table where the head honcho, wearing a bowler hat, was sitting and staring directly at him.

Carefully, the man facing him opened up a thick manila folder and broke the silence in a low baritone voice.

"I see you've had a full career," he muttered to himself.

"Yes," Bob managed. "But who are you? Why am I hear? I want to talk to my attorney!"

"Carlos De Maria Vartoulez Gomez Sanchez de Banillelo," came the answer, to only one of Bob's questions.

"Okay."

"Mr. McConnell, our file here indicates that you have some valuable information to which we want access. We have familiarity with the US and Canadian coal industry, but we want to know more about the oil industry."

By now, the person he was talking to was sounding more and more like a member of some Spanish-speaking mafia. Bob's palms began to sweat and his heart quickened.

"Listen, sir, I just started my foray into this industry. My knowledge is limited."

What Bob was saying was true, to an extent. While he had done his due diligence and been reading up recently on the oil industry, he still had lots to learn about CanGas's operations.

"Look here, son," said Carlos, his accent thick as ever. "We form the junta. We are the People's Resistance Front of Colombia. Our amigos are all over South and Central America. We deal in hundreds of thousands of dollars in cocaine and marijuana trade on a daily basis. You don't want to mess with us, eh, Martinez?"

Carlos's compatriot nodded his head, as if not giving the action much thought at all.

Bob was insistent. "Well, what do you want? Just get me out of here!"

"Very simple, my friend." The grin Carlos had on his face was wide like that of the Cheshire cat. "We want two things: cash and corporate information."

***

Martha was hysterical. She had called the cops. However, unbeknown to her, the Ontario Provincial Police, the RCMP and even Interpol were on the case since it involved the abduction of the CEO of one of the biggest companies in Canada.

CBC and CTV, the national networks, had blasted the story on their nightly six o'clock news reports. The race was on to find Bob.

According to the work carried out by the RCMP and Interpol, in conjunction with the US Central Intelligence Agency (CIA) and MI6 in the United Kingdom, a lead surfaced as to Bob's whereabouts. It was believed that Bob was being held hostage at an undisclosed location in Mexico, just south of the Texas border.

But Martha had discovered some sad news. When she was rummaging through some of Bob's belongings the other day, she came across an old journal of his from the war period. In it Bob wrote about having got a young English girl from Kent pregnant, before he met Martha, right in the middle of the war.

Another interesting discovery occurred when Martha discovered a love letter written to Bob, stuffed in his journal. The letter was not written by her—it was from another woman!

Dearest Bob,

I am doing well, and I don't have much time to write this. I want you to know that your son had a wonderful time in celebrating his ninth birthday. Hope we can see each other soon!

Love,

Julie

His son, who by Martha's calculation should be around twenty, was eager to meet his biological father and had even taken on Bob's last name—McConnell. Martha felt betrayed and was livid. How could Bob have kept this secret affair and child from her?

After a period of intense negotiation, Bob was finally released to CIA officials in the Hilton Hotel in Miami. The Mexican druglords were planning on staying in that city at an undisclosed resort—a vacation destination—with some of their amigos. CanGas agreed to pay $1 million and provide a few copies of business documents to the junta in exchange for Bob's safety.

The good news was that all of the documents provided to the junta were simply statistics that were available in CanGas's annual report. The RCMP was greatly indebted to the CIA, as well as MI6, who although were not able to prosecute the junta at the time of Bob's release, the crime-stopping organizations had gathered crucial information for future international cooperation in stopping the evil work of this group. The junta, with its intricacies and interconnectedness to other criminal groups, would require much cooperation and lots of resources on the part of crime enforcement agencies to stop them.

Part II: Energized

Chapter 1

Fifty-two years later

"I can't handle it anymore!" exclaimed Josh.

Josh McConnell had been unemployed from the oil industry for nearly a year. With three young mouths to feed at home, he wasn't sure how much longer he could make ends meet. McConnell was of average build and sported a recently acquired beard that his girlfriend did not fully appreciate. She found it scratched her face too much when he swooped down for a kiss.

Another nagging feeling he had was that he would not be able to pay his alimony, which was substantial, given the fact that his employment insurance was due to run out any day now. He was saddened about his divorce. Josh came from a reasonably strong family himself, but he recently found out that his father was born out of wedlock, a topic which was not broached too often by family members.

Nevertheless, Josh was thankful that it was almost December and that his parents always gave him a generous financial gift at Christmastime. That was surprisingly sacrificial given that his folks owned a modest fishery in Newfoundland. Thankfully, cod fishing had picked up again in the past few years since its collapse in 1992.

"Can you help me tie up my shoes?" asked Josh's youngest daughter, Jordan. She was precocious, but her manual dexterity wasn't as developed as her two older sisters.

"How come Dad said, 'I can't do it anymore'?" Jenna, the middle child, at age eight still didn't grasp the financial bind her father was in as he sought to put bread on the table in the middle of an economic downturn.

"Come on!" yelled Ashleigh. Josh's eldest was starting to get impatient as she waited outside for the rest of her family to hurry up so they could attend her piano recital, for which she had practised for months. Ashleigh knew that her endless rehearsals of Vivaldi's *Four Seasons* was going to pay off real soon.

Josh scrambled to help Jordan with her shoes as he gestured to his other two children to get in the pickup truck. "Never mind what I mean about not being able to handle *it* anymore," Josh muttered, almost breathlessly, as he tried to get his other two kids out the door.

As Josh started his truck, he still couldn't shake the feeling that he wasn't doing a good enough job of looking for work and trying to provide for his young family.

***

The white Chevy Silverado pulled up to the St. Andrew's Presbyterian Church parking lot. There hadn't been too much snow this year, which was unusual for Edmonton. Could it be global warming, the phenomenon that the environmentalists were going on about for years? Josh was always amazed how much snow he'd seen when he worked up in Fort McMurray. There was so much snow that they had to spend a significant amount of time clearing it off the rigs in the middle of winter. "If only I were still up there working for EnOil Inc.," thought Josh, shrugging his shoulders. "But that wouldn't have changed my marriage."

As he corralled his girls through the big solid-oak doors, Josh thought back to this day, twelve years ago, when he was married in the very same church. Life seemed so much simpler back then. At the time, he had recently landed a lucrative job drilling oil in northern Alberta. He was marrying an attractive young lady from his hometown. He was all-around starting a new life. What more could he ask for? What could go wrong? Life was good.

Well, apparently a lot could go wrong. Over the years and as their family grew, Josh felt the pressures of life creeping up on him. This all happened just like the Biblical parable about the seed and the sower—the worries of life seemed to choke Josh just like the bramble in the bush. It wasn't just the fact that he spent long hours at work in Fort McMurray; it was the stress of keeping up with the Joneses as he slowly worked his way up the corporate ladder. Nearly all one hundred employees at EnOil had at least one boat, a supernice house and usually one or more beamers or Mercedes. As Josh aged, he realized that just because he had worked his way up to a six-figure salary, it didn't necessitate him having to spend it all. Although, the cost of living in Fort Mac was pretty insane.

But now all Josh had to worry about was pleasing his talented daughter, Ashleigh. Josh and the other two girls found their way to seats at the back of the church. At least Ashleigh's performance was at the end of the evening. That meant he didn't have to feel bad about arriving right on time, as the first music student made his way up to the piano. Ashleigh, as discretely as possible, walked up the side of the church to the stage, looking almost as if she had lost her confidence. She hated being late and had being looking forward to this evening for a long time.

***

It was so embarrassing. Josh was living off welfare and was barely paying the bills. He had taken his three girls to the local soup kitchen. The building looked almost cavernous. It was located in the basement of an old stone Mennonite church.

Since Josh had been coming for a few weeks, he was starting to feel like a regular around this place. His daughters were young enough to not question why they were coming here, why it was necessary and why daddy didn't have a job like all their friends' daddies at school. The family was living in a poor inner-city neighbourhood that had experienced significant crime in the last few years. The house they were living in was subsidized and decrepit, built in the 1920s. They caught more mice than they'd like to in the house. The cat they had was useless!

The situation was extremely difficult—Josh hadn't yet mustered up the nerve to explain to any of his daughters that he had been let go from his well-paying job and had been out of work for months. He still left the house at seven-fifteen each morning and went to the local employment centre to look for jobs. The centre had helped him prepare his resume and cover letter and had given him interview tips that would help him in landing an offer of employment. The economy in Alberta was horrendous. Even people working at the local grocery stores or Tim Hortons were losing their jobs.

Fortunately, Josh and his fledgling family now lived in Edmonton, where the ravages of the tanking economy, caused by a sinking loonie and low oil prices, hadn't quite hit him as hard as in the more northern parts of the province. After all, on top of being a government town, Edmonton's economy was more diversified. Its refining and petrochemical companies were not always decisively affected by swings in the oil prices. Nevertheless, this time the city was also affected in a devastating way. The economy was comparable to the dust bowl of the 1930s, the era of the Great Depression. At a national level, the country's banks and investors were being dragged down by a global drying up of demand for oil, or *black gold* as they called it, which had been the staple of the Western economy for decades. More generally, there was a sinking demand for natural resources that were once greatly needed to fuel the growth of rising powers like China.

Chapter 2

Denise helped unload the minivan in a hurry. She had been dating Josh for the better part of six months now, not too long after he had lost his job as an oil worker. I'm so glad he's not messy, she reflected, as she started to put the groceries away. Her previous boyfriend, Ron, was about as messy as they come. This was no word of a lie: any of her friends were quick to admit that not only was Ron a bad procrastinator, but he had a nasty habit of not bothering to put his dirty clothes in the hamper and keeping about every piece of clutter imaginable. "Train up a child in the way he should go, and when he is old he will not depart from it," is what her mother always told Denise, but she wasn't always so sure of it when it came to some people—at least not with Ron.

But Josh was different than the rest. Life had dealt him a difficult hand, but he refused to be affected by it. His ex-wife had been unfaithful to him one year into the marriage, and the habit and it still stung years later after the children were born. The pain of Josh's separation still stung. Phhewww! Denise almost said aloud as she finally put the last grocery away in the crisper. I wouldn't have wanted to have been in a marriage like that…At least Josh had won custody of the children for most of the time, thank goodness.

Ever since the Oka Crisis, Christopher Crywolf had wanted to make a difference. He wanted to make an impact on Canadian society at large, not just the Mohawk of Akwesasne First Nation. His family was a mishmash of many different Indigenous groups: Beothuk from the Newfoundland, Mi'kmaq from Nova Scotia and Squamish from British Columbia. Chris did not like he belonged to any one nation distinguishably. He had a tan-coloured skin and his hair was jet black, with a streak of white running through it.

His ex-wife was part Cree and Haida; his daughter was dating a teenaged boy from Iqaluit. If this were a couple of hundred years ago, Crywolf's families may have may not have gotten along with each other.

Thankfully, this was not the case today. Crywolf had determined that he would become a lawyer. And not just any attorney–but a successful one that would make a mark on Canadian society.

Chris Crywolf followed in the footsteps of his father, Leonard Crywolf. His dad was no lawyer like himself, but he was a big achiever, having conducted highly sensitive and important work on behalf of the Canadian government before the Iron Curtain fell in 1991. Like his father, Chris wanted to leave a legacy that would make his children's children proud.

He had started off his career actually representing his aunts and uncles, who had been victims of the horrible residential schools. Thankfully, Crywolf was starting to see currents of Canadian perspectives changing on the issue. Was the government going to pay recompense and own up to this terrible injustice and sin of the past?

None of this mattered now…Crywolf needed to concentrate on the case he had on hand. He was helping a client with his divorce. What could he say? Although it wasn't his specialty, his other business was drying up.Soon, though, he would be able to get back to the work he was meant to do—helping his people seek the justice they deserved.

As the children came home from school, Denise could hear the hum of the school bus take off. "Good to see you all," she exclaimed joyfully as she hugged and kissed each one of them. Ashleigh was a little reluctant to get kissed, but the other two girls were delighted.

As his car pulled into the driveway, Josh was so thankful to have Denise as a girlfriend. He appreciated the small ways that Denise cared for him, the way she treated each of his children with so much love and attention.

"Any luck at the Strathcona Job Fair?" Denise had a hint of optimism in her voice, which was exactly what Josh was seeking as he walked into the rented duplex, holding an extralarge Tim Hortons coffee in hand. He was happy that it was still Roll Up the Rim season—maybe he'd win something like a new flat screen TV, or even a RAV4. Heaven knew he'd appreciate a new television set. You could start to see a tinge of pink on the top left-hand corner of the television screen, which had been acquired at a garage sale. His old house in Fort McMurray hadn't fetched a good selling price—he was just lucky to have sold it at all with the collapse of the economy in Alberta. Hopefully things would turn around for the better soon.

"I've gotta get to work, love!" Denise was nearly out the door by the time Josh put his coat away. "Time waits for no man…or woman, for that matter." Josh caught a wry smile on Denise's face as she zipped up her high-heeled boots, the type that were really à la mode, and rushed to her Jeep in the driveway.

Josh flipped on the tube. At this time in the afternoon, the soap operas were over and the shows geared to children, freshly back from their school day, were starting. Not really certain what he was searching for, Josh mindlessly flipped through the channels—maybe there was something worth watching. He didn't watch TV too often; there wasn't much on these days. Josh was trying to numb the pain of not finding a job and assuage his fear of not being able to find another decent job. He was amazed at how television had changed so much over the past few years: there was hardly a program on TV that wasn't a reality show! He smiled as he thought about how much Denise enjoyed reality television. The last time he watched TV was when he couldn't sleep the other night.

"Girls—go do your homework!" Josh leaned over the sofa as he hollered the instructions upstairs. Silence. He wasn't sure if that meant that his girls were already doing their homework or if they were distracted by Instagram. Josh really had to crack down on their social media use lately. Ashleigh was into everything—Facebook, Twitter, Instagram, YouTube—you name it, she liked it. Her younger sisters were quickly learning about all these apps from her. Ten going on twenty-six, Ashleigh was on track academically, but Josh had to make sure she didn't get too boy-crazy. That's why he was consistently encouraging her to play the piano and soccer. I've got to keep my kids focused, he told himself. Otherwise, there's so many distractions in life that will keep them from success.

As Josh flipped off the television, the doorbell rang. I've got to spend my time doing something more productive, he convinced himself, as he walked to the door, thankful for the interruption.

"Surprise!" Erma gave him a sloppy wet kiss, jovial lady she was, with a few extra pounds around her midsection since the last time he saw her. Good grief, Josh caught himself thinking. How come my ex-in-laws are still a part of my life? Oh yeah, it's the children. Plus they thought Josh was more responsible than their own daughter. Tony gave Josh a firm handshake and a slap on his back, the type that coaches give to players before they go on the field. Tony was broad-shouldered but was in good physical shape for his age.

"You brought some homemade pie—lemon meringue—it's the girls' favourite! Awesome," Josh exclaimed as he hung the heavy coats up in the closet. This was the third time in the last week his in-laws had visited him and his children. Perhaps it was because his father-in-law had just retired. Perhaps it was because it was Jordan's birthday last Tuesday. He wasn't quite certain, but hopefully the frequency of visits would diminish.

At any rate, at least Josh was set for dinner. His mother-in-law made a delectable casserole! Josh could almost taste the crusty, cheesy broccoli and tuna-filled dish. His mouth started to salivate.

Erma and Tony tag-teamed the dinner preparation as Josh neatly set the table. Ashleigh, Jenna and Jordan wandered down the stairs. Could they move any slower? Josh thought. Once downstairs, Jenna and Jordan began to do cartwheels as Ashleigh practised the piano.

Josh cracked open a beer. On second thought, maybe it wasn't such a good idea to drink alcohol. He had a hockey game within an hour, and he wanted to be alert for the game. As he sat down on the plaid armchair watching his beautiful girls pursuing their hobbies, he suddenly had an idea about a job prospect.

Chapter 3

As Josh skated back and forth on the ice, he couldn't help but continue to think about his job search. He was on the ice doing slapshots, gritting his teeth, convincing himself that the latest idea was a good one.

What had got him thinking about this particular opportunity was his disdain for sporadic construction work this past summer. As Josh passed the puck vigorously to Jeff Watkins, his long-time hockey buddy, he remembered the dog days of summer, when he was out roofing in the sun for hours on end. He could taste the sweat as he worked on that roof, baking in the sunlight—the same perspiration he experienced as he was doing laps on the ice. Josh recalled Jimmy Bennett, his other hockey buddy, telling him about his line of work over beers the other week. It had to do with manufacturing and installing solar panels. Bennett was a heavy-set man in his early forties with thick-rimmed glasses and a goatee. Although life had thrown him its fair share of challenges, he seemed to always manage to have a smile on his face.

Renewable energy, like solar, was becoming increasingly ubiquitous, especially in places like Europe. Even China was starting to develop clean energy goals—a welcomed development. It was not surprising when word got out that Barack Obama had vetoed TransCanada's Keystone XL pipeline. Besides Obamacare, clean energy was a cornerstone of the current American presidency. There was still the Northern Gateway and Energy East pipelines, but with the low price of oil, there was less political clout to leverage for the big oil companies to lobby for pipelines. Besides, much of Quebec vehemently opposed Energy East as if it were evil, and the Northern Gateway was bogged down in government approvals and regulations. Yet liquefied natural gas was of interest to Quebec, in the Saguenay. This goes to show the province was definitely open to other energy alternatives besides "dirty oil." Both the Northern Gateway and the Energy East pipelines were bogged down from moving ahead with administrative government procedures due to the First Nations' resistance to their development, although the conciliatory approach adopted by Prime Minister Justin Trudeau was reassuring.

There were several reasons for the resistance, but First Nations claimed that the pipelines infringed upon their homeland. Hopefully, if the pipelines were built, Indigenous people would be employed in building and maintaining the pipelines. But there were also concerns about the potential environmental hazards of having pipelines. There was truth to the environmental concerns; however, experts would attest to the fact that pipelines were significantly safer than all the transport of oil by rail that had been occurring in Canada and the United States.

Also, there had been quite an advancement in drone capability over the last few years that would be able to inspect these pipelines to make sure they were safe. Accidents *did* indeed happen, but all told, given the current network of liquefied and natural gas pipelines, such as those owned by Kinder Morgan, in North America, it could be argued that they were by far safer than transporting crude oil by train.

Nevertheless, there were different lines of thought when it came to pipelines. Some people, such as Josh's father, thought that Canada should have more refineries rather than shipping as much raw bitumen as possible by truck or pipeline to the large US refineries, such as in Texas, just to have the product shipped back in the form of gasoline and other refined petrochemical products. From an economics standpoint, apparently many people thought that it made more sense to have the product refined in the United States. Since there were already a lot of refineries there due to economies of scale, it would be cheaper to do the job on their side of the border.

But the cost to Canada was the loss of good-paying jobs. While Canadian oil companies might have racked up temporary profits extracting the crude oil from the ground, American companies would benefit from all of the jobs for folks processing and refining the product in US refineries. It was even an NDP campaign promise in the previous federal election that the party would help ensure that additional Canadian refineries were built and maintained if their party was elected to power.

Regardless of where one stood when it came to the topic of pipelines, Canada needed to diversify its economy. The East and the West never seemed to run in sync: when the West did well, the East was having a downturn. The converse was true: when the East did well, the West had a slumping economy. Former prime minister Stephen Harper, having been adopted into the Alberta fold, captivating a swath of the Reformed Party base and reinvigorating the Conservative Party with his rhetoric and strategy, was a very strong supporter of the economic development of the oil fields during his decade in power. Prime Minister Trudeau's reception out West was less warm, in part due to the acrimony caused by his father's National Energy Program of the 1970s.

Some of Josh's friends knew Stephen Harper and loved his policies. They wanted government to get out of the way and simply create good policies for the industry, not work its way into it. *Neocons,* as they referred to themselves. Most of them, at one time or another, campaigned for the Conservative Party. But alas, those days were over for now. Rachel Notley, the NDP provincial premier, had an unequivocal attraction to renewable energy. And if she could win an election on such a platform, then surely there was a base in Alberta that stood alongside her in the belief that there were alternate sources of energy to harness, other than what the tar sands have to offer, with all of its bad publicity. Celebrities like Leonardo DiCaprio and Neil Young challenged the idea that developing the oil sands was a good one.

Josh thought deeply about the pitch the oil companies were making to the federal government. He could hardly believe it! They were asking the government to earmark money in the upcoming budget to fill in some of the excess oil wells. Truthfully, Josh would much rather do this work than any other job on earth. Even before he made his way up to the fancy managerial position in Calgary, which he had had before he was let go, he loved the hard, manual labour of working on the oil rigs. He even loved the air up in Fort McMurray, for all its so-called pollution, which was surprising given that the work was believed to be so "dirty" by environmentalists.

But this idea of a new job that Bennett had gotten Josh hooked on—installing solar panels—was a good second best in terms of a career. Josh was always good with his hands, and Bennett convinced him that renewable energy was the way of the future. To think that Alberta would ever fully embrace energy production apart from the oil industry was almost unimaginable. I guess this was what the NDP party was trying to sell the province; that the economy needed to diversify more from the traditional sources of wealth that were generated from oil revenues.

At any rate, oil certainly wasn't anywhere near $120 a barrel as it was just a couple of years ago. Those oil prices kept the previous Conservative government's coffers plenty full. With oil being as low as $30 a barrel these days, there wasn't much hope of building an economy on that resource. There was even talk on CBC about the possibility of reinstating a provincial sales tax! Incredible, but Josh could picture it happening. Especially now, with the province making more money on liquor sales than exports of raw bitumen. Crazy times—former premier of Alberta Ralph Klein would be rolling in his grave.

Anyways, Josh was getting psyched at the idea of using his hands to make a living by installing solar panels, one house (or business) at a time. As soon as the hockey game was over, he skipped going out for nachos with his buddies so that he could race home to tuck his children into bed and kiss them goodnight. The thought crossed his mind about how much he would miss his girls when he took them to be with their mother for the next week. Then he hurried downstairs to his laptop.

"Renewable energy…solar panels" Josh typed into Google. Maybe that would work. Once he had learned a bit of the basics of the technology and how popular it was becoming, he proceeded to his next search: "Jobs…solar panels…Edmonton area." Slowly, Josh began to realize just how much potential there was in this burgeoning field. People were really getting into this renewable energy idea…even in redneck Alberta! Josh let out a sigh of relief. He could even visualize himself in work clothes, hard boots and all, succeeding in this profession. The more Josh researched the subject, the more convinced he became that promoting renewable energy was something he wanted to do for a living.

Nelson Gotlieb listened as the water pitter-pattered along the windowsill. He was still trying to figure out how to write the code for this neat new computer program he was concocting.

Ever since the early 1990s, Gotlieb had a keen fascination with computers. He had the hunched-over appearance of a programmer, and liked to keep his hair well-trimmed. Everyone in his family was a nerd, too. Back when his father worked at IBM, everyone wore blue suits, ties and horn-rimmed glasses. They had names like E. B. Surrey, F. A. Martin or S. A. Williams. Women were secretaries or nurses.

Now, everything had changed. In the closing years of the twenty-first century, women had been breaking the glass ceiling of the workplace for over twenty years. Khakis, polo shirts and sweaters were replacing the suit. Sports jackets were donned for the more formal occasions.

None of the outward trappings of businesspeople mattered to Gotlieb, though. Formal or informal, what he cared about was programming. C++, Basic, Java—you name it—he was interested in it and learned how to code it. He could recite computer programs—backward—in his sleep. It was no mystery: God had created him to program computers. His whole family loved technology. His grandfather had been a Russian spy who defected to Canada after the Second World War.

Gotlieb worked for a high-tech company in Kanata. This company was at the forefront of fibre optics. Nextus Techologies was in the big league—competing with the likes of Nortel. As he was writing a computer program for how a Smarthome could be programmed to control a house's climate and its energy usage, synced with solar panels, he had to find an edge that would cut out his primary competitor: Bennett Solar.

Chapter 4

Just before sunrise—Saturday, December 19, 2015—West Edmonton Mall neighbourhood

Josh's parents' gift came early this year. Perhaps he should have spent it on his daughters, but his parents understood that he needed time away from family obligations once in a while, even when he was unemployed. Even though there was less snow this year, there was still enough for skiing, and it was a good thing, since Banff so heavily relied on the tourism industry.

Jimmy Bennett met Josh at the local Tim Hortons at six o'clock. Josh was a skier, and Bennett was a snowboarder. Their time spent skiing had a dual purpose—they were going to discuss Josh's job of installing solar panels starting in the springtime, and they were going to have fun. Bennett was looking to hire, and Josh's technical know-how and work ethic were the right mix. The two had become buddies since Josh had replied to the online add that Bennett had recently posted on his company's website. The strange thing was that they had known each other already as acquaintances from hockey. Even though Bennett ran what was considered now to be a large company, he nevertheless still interviewed and took the time to get to know most of the people they hired. It was a factor that contributed to the company's overall success, as well as ensuring the quality of the new recruits.

The coffee tasted smooth as Josh took a sip and bantered with Bennett about their families and the weather. It was so nice to escape to go skiing once in a while. His girls were at a gymnastics competition with Bennett's wife and children along with Denise, so he knew they were going to have an awesome day.

As Bennett's Dodge Durango SUV took off from Tim Hortons with Josh and all their gear, the winter tires spun, and it wasn't just caused by the newly minted snow. "You always drive like this?" Josh chortled as managed to wolf down his breakfast sandwich.

"Believe me, I don't try; it comes naturally," replied Bennett as he took another bite of his hash brown, which he was trying to eat while driving, a bad move indeed.

As they set off on the two-hour trip to Banff, the sun rose stunningly over the horizon. It felt like a glimmer of heaven coming down onto the cold windswept earth. Just then, Josh felt a pull at his heartstrings—he remembered the faith he espoused as a child. There was something in those breathtaking views he saw that echoed of the supernatural.

He grew up in a strict Baptist household where the word "fun" seemed to be missing from his parents' vocabulary. As Josh got older, he wandered from the faith. At thirty-five, his parents wondered if he was ever going to turn back. His young adult years were marred by too much marijuana, alcohol and even crack cocaine. Through rehabilitation and by the grace of God, he had been able to break free from his addiction. Josh had attended Teen Ranch, but the gospel introduced to him there didn't really stick to him. Like the prodigal son, he was plain-old rebellious during his younger years—only he hadn't really returned to his faith. He became more faintly aware that there was a gaping vacuum of nothingness in his life that left him feeling helpless and out of control.

"You said you're a Christian, right?" Josh could hardly believe he was asking this question. He had pushed spiritual questions out of his mind until now.

"You bet," Bennett said in stark contrast to Josh's parents. Though both Bennett and Josh's parents espoused the same faith, Bennett was not hypocritical in living out his faith.

"It's gonna be an *amazing* day for skiing. The snow conditions are excellent." The abrupt way that Josh changed the very conversation he started was startling even to himself. His brashness was uncharacteristic, but the topic of faith would have to wait until another time.

***

Josh and Bennett zoomed down the hills of Mount Norquay. Smaller than Lake Louise or Sunshine Village, Norquay was no less majestic. What's more, parts of Norquay, warned Josh's father, were significantly more difficult to ski than the other two mountains nearby. Certain peaks were never groomed, and the pitches could be staggering. The view from the top of the runs was absolutely stunning, and the air was fresh and crisp. You could see mountains for miles that were covered with beautiful evergreen trees, cascading down the sides of the mountains like waterfalls.

Looking forward to a hot chocolate break, Josh scooted down the hill with Bennett. Later, he would try his hand at skiing the highest hills the mountain had to offer. I've taken my share of lessons before, as a child, he reasoned. I can conquer the most challenging hills this mountain has to offer, no problem.

Josh headed into the chalet, ordered his hot chocolate and sat down to relax with Bennett. It was incredible how many Aussies there were working in the Rocky Mountains! Second to only Germans, these folks outnumbered native Canadians by a high ratio. Josh recalled hearing that there was some agreement between Australia and Canada that allowed a favourable work visa arrangement. Known for their enjoyment of world travelling, a lot of German youth also worked in the Rockies. In the past, it had been a requirement for them to have a year-long military service or volunteering experience, and many Germans went to another country for this, as an opportunity to sneak some travel time in.

After their break, the two friends summited the mountain again, this time on the highest peak, and stood in awe. The mountainous view was accented by brilliant sunlight bouncing off of the pristine snow.

"Isn't God's creation incredible?" offered up Bennett, taking it in all around him.

"Yeah, it sure is," Josh caught himself saying.

Next thing Josh knew, Bennett was zooming down the expert hill, carving sharp patterns all the way to the base.

"I better hurry up," Josh said to himself.

***

Tumbling. That's all Josh could think about. Falling, rolling, gliding steadily down the side of the mountain…and picking up speed. He recalled bending over to take off his skis to move to safer ground at the top of the hill, and then he free-fell with skis and poles popping off as he descended the steep mountain terrain. It was like a winter waterslide, made thick by the hard ice densely packed into the ground. Some parts of the moguls were so slick that you could see the dirt ground under the hill.

The terrain had been difficult to read due to the freezing and thawing that had occurred the last couple of months with the swings in the temperature. There were moguls on either side of Josh; he was afraid to plant his feet down firmly in the ground lest that would cause him to fly through the air at high speed. Josh found himself reciting a few supplicatory prayers and being very thankful that he had rented a helmet.

Finally, he stopped falling and could hear the reassuring call of the ski patroller. Josh could see a few snowboarders whizzing by him in his peripheral vision. "Are you okay?" came a muffled voice from behind him.

Josh looked up, as if in a daze. He was so thankful for the ski patroller. She casually skied down to him with his poles and skis. "Can you make it to the bottom of the hill?" she queried. He could but would be grateful to have a beer to calm his nerves. After all, he had finished skiing for the day!

***

Jordan, Ashleigh and Jenna were having a blast at the gymnastics competition. More accurately, Jenna and Jordan were enjoying competing in gymnastics while Ashleigh ogled at and flirted with the boys from her class. I'm almost eleven, she thought. It's not too young to think about guys. Ashleigh was a smart cookie and had top grades, especially in math and science. She was a favourite among her teachers.

Ann, Bennett's wife, was thoroughly enjoying the competition as well. She was so glad to spend time with Denise. Despite not having children of her own, Denise was a natural with them. Also, Ann remembered, she was a Christian. What a blessing! It is always good to have more Christian women in my life, she reflected. I'm so glad Denise is studying to be a social worker—she'll be so good at it. She studies so hard and deserves a rewarding career helping other people tackle some of their personal problems. Christians need to have people like her who are able to speak truth into their lives and vice versa.

Chapter 5

Now that Josh and Bennett had finished their full day of skiing, they settled into one of Banff's fine local eateries, a pub called Randy's, where the booze flowed freely and the company was always friendly. They could finally talk shop and discuss Josh's future job, to see if it was the right fit.

"Well, that's been quite a day of snowboarding…or skiing, in your case." Bennett looked truly rejuvenated after a day on the slopes.

Josh smiled. "Yeah, it sure has been. As much as I regret falling down the hill, I'm determined to go to Whistler one day. Thankfully, although I have a few bruises, I don't feel like I have any broken bones or fractures."

"I think you've got the right attitude. But maybe you should get checked to make sure you're really okay?"

"Nah…I'll be fine."

Soon, Bennett was ready to cut to the chase and talk to Josh about business.

"Renewable energy is the next big growth area for jobs," Bennett started off, in between a mouthful of fries.

"Really?" Josh said in between a gulp of beer and a bite of wings. He knew a little about the topic from his preliminary research, and he was mostly convinced that Bennett was right.

"Yeah," continued Bennett, "I don't think I ever told you that's what I did my PhD dissertation on—how renewable energy, like wind, solar panels and thermal energy, will have a positive effect on the economy and job creation."

"Get out!" He had always remembered Bennett as a bit of a party animal who appeared not to have time for books or studies.

"You bet," Bennett retorted. "I'm proposing you come to work for me in British Columbia."

"British Columbia? What about Edmonton?"

"I know. I've thought it through, though. The job growth in this industry is mostly in BC for now. There's a cluster of renewable energy companies in that province, especially near Vancouver. It'll change soon enough, I'm sure, and then later we could always open up shop in Edmonton."

"Does that mean we get to go skiing at Whistler?" You could see the excitement in Josh's face as he said this. He had also heard about Kicking Horse Mountain near Golden—another great place that was recommended for skiers. The Champagne Powder capital of the world or something.

"Of course, that's part of the fun of it! The province is a hip place—it's a Canadian technological hub, an environmentally friendly city. Being closer to Asia than the rest of Canada, it takes advantage of this unique trade opportunity as a competitive advantage."

As Bennett described the phenomenal transformation of the renewable energy industry, how many homeowners were installing solar panels to become self-sufficient, or partially self-sufficient, Josh devoured the last bites of his wings. In his earlier research, he came across the name of the business magnate Elon Musk—the owner of Tesla and learned about his investment in SolarCity and small, efficient batteries that would store energy for homeowners. It was fascinating to consider how the market for renewable energy was increasing. No wonder, considering all the challenges of the oil industry. Quebec's Lac-Mégantic disaster of July 2013 had taught everyone the riskiness of transporting oil in Canada, especially by rail, although pipeline transport was far from perfect. But there was an overall sense that people were thirsting for more environmentally friendly energy—solar, wind, geothermal, you name it; renewable energy was in!

***

It was ten in the morning on a Boxing Day, which happened to fall on a Saturday this year. Josh was talking to his father, Norm. His father never called him at this hour. At least not normally. But this was Christmas; things were different. Norm had lost literally thousands of dollars in oil investments, so he was overjoyed that Josh was looking outside of his former career path to put bread on the table. Due to the money that Norm had lost this year in his investments, he had decided that he and his wife would stay in

Newfoundland for the holiday season. But it wasn't all bad news. Hopefully, Josh and his girls could visit them during the March break, when Norm was hoping to profit from a new invention he had recently patented.

Josh always loved talking with his father. An electrical engineer by trade, Norm had a penchant for designing machines. His latest patent was a sophisticated version of an unmanned aerial vehicle (UAV), which was a piece of technology that was rapidly becoming popular. Specifically, Norm had designed a low-cost UAV that would assist farmers in monitoring their crops, so as to ensure they weren't ravaged by rodents or other pests. The biggest market for this UAV would likely be in the midwestern United States, places like Iowa, where there were huge tracts of cornfields. However, there were several other places in Canadian Prairies that were promising for future sales. Another place that UAVs were being used a lot was the military. The idea was that there would be less casualties of war with their use.

Norm always said that an engineer was taught first and foremost how to solve problems. There was no disputing that. Perhaps Josh should have studied engineering instead of software development, but it was too late for that change at this juncture in his life, with three young mouths to feed at home. Maybe his career would have been more stable, more upwardly mobile, or he could have had an even higher paying job working in the oil field, but with all the recent ruptures and uncertainties in the global economy over the last several years, he doubted that. At any rate, now that Josh had the prospect of a stable job working for Bennett, he was just plain thankful. He didn't care for being the richest man on the block. He just wanted to provide sufficiently for his family.

Chapter 6

Sunny weekday in April 2016

Josh worked doggedly at installing the solar panels on the huge mansion just outside of Kelowna, British Columbia. He had never known how picturesque a province it was with the Rocky Mountains and all. Josh had never been there before…he'd only heard about it second-hand from some friends. I guess the licence plate motto says it all: Beautiful BC, Josh thought to himself.

Josh had made a few key friends in his new career at Bennett Solar. It had helped, too, that he worked with some men, such as Bennett, with children roughly the same age as his children. He was grateful for this connection. He was even more grateful that his his ex-wife had also moved to Kelowna and found a well-paying job at a start-up there. That way, both parents could continue to easily see their children.

Kelowna was a more appealing place than Josh thought it would be. He was even wondering if he wanted to return to Edmonton long term after all. His children had made new friends in a wonderful school nearby, and Denise had found work as a social worker at a private Christian practice, now that she had finished her studies. The Okanagan Valley was alluring, with its incredible vineyards and breathtaking views. Another rush of gratitude overwhelmed Josh. The more he thought about it, the more he wanted to spend the foreseeable future in BC.

The warm sun was refreshing on Josh's back, and he felt as if he were a roofer most of the time. The typical solar panels were installed on house roofs or high up on the side of a building. Even with the sun beaming down, the April weather betrayed a coolness that made it seem like Old Man Winter was reticent to be gone. Josh rubbed his hands back and forth to warm them up in between screwing in the panels. He had to make sure he didn't fall off the roof, but with his good boots and excellent balance, the likelihood of that happening was remote. Sometimes, if the pitch of the roof was really bad, he would be fastened on with a safety harness.

Compared to the grunt work of roofing, Josh found installing solar panels to be a welcomed improvement. Roofing was more gruelling—it was back-breaking, physically demanding work. Roofers had to work very efficiently. They started at the crack of dawn and resumed work after the peak of the heat of midday.

Josh was also thankful that he wasn't operating a jackhammer for a living. He knew a few of his buddies from high school who went on to work in construction, and a couple of them worked on city contracts, having to use a jackhammer to tear up the pavement or concrete for a work project. It would be forty-degree weather sometimes in the summer, and these guys would be sweating buckets, clad with heavy coveralls and big, heavy steel-toed boots. The pay was half-decent, but Josh doubted he could handle that sort of work day in, day out.

With this cooler April weather, Josh got to thinking: could Bennett Solar still carry out its work come next winter? Was there work to be done in this field of employment when the temperature turned cold? Josh had thoroughly enjoyed the winter weather in British Columbia since moving there in January. He went on a brief ski trip at Whistler with his family and thoroughly enjoyed skating on outdoor rinks. Nevertheless, Josh had to make sure that he had enough money when the solar panel installation season ended.

Sitting in the magnificent Alliance Church in Westbank, originally planted by an offshoot of the denomination from Chilliwack, many thoughts were going through Josh's head. Were the preacher's words reliable? How could he be trusted to deliver *the truth*? What was the truth? Josh thought he was living in a postmodern age where anything went, as long as it didn't impinge on the rights of other people. In the current age of moral relativism, it was difficult to agree on anything, at least not anything of substance. These were the sorts of existential questions with which Josh was wrestling.

Ever since Ashleigh started attending the church's youth group, there was a draw in Josh's heart to know more about what *the church* was all about. There was something captivating for Ashleigh in the youth group. The games were fun, and soon enough she started inviting her own school friends along to attend. The youth pastor always found a way to link current events to Biblical realities.

Jordan and Jenna were also starting to get immersed in Sunday school as Josh and Denise started attending the church more regularly. Denise had moved nearby to Josh, but on principle—as a devout Christian—had opted to live with a roommate for the time being. Josh, meanwhile, was seriously considering proposing to her soon. She had irresistible qualities: gentleness, meekness, tenderness. She had boundaries, was principled, and wasn't about to give herself away until she was married.

 Although the church was not quite in the Fraser Valley Bible belt, it was influenced by that community to a large extent. It had been started a dozen years ago with only fifty people, located halfway between Peachland and Summerland, in an old rundown barn. Far from a Langley, which was home of the Vineyard and Focus on the Family Canada, Northgate Alliance Church had grown to several thousand members. The church soon moved to the Westbank suburb of Kelowna, into a sprawling building with a modern, eclectic architectural design and a large parking lot. The preacher must have been doing something right—he had *the anointing*, as charismatics liked to call it. Or was it that the Spirit of God was moving, as Denise had pointed out on a few occasions?

 Josh paid attention to Jenna's Cub Scout program as well, which also encouraged a spiritual component through the Religion in Life badge. He also appreciated the fact that Cubs were encouraged to "do their best" and to do good turns daily. These were important parts of becoming good citizens of the country and, more generally, the world.

But something was different about Pastor Duddley. He preached with such conviction and gusto! The claims of Jesus made about his own divinity were unparalleled in Josh's personal investigation of the world's major religions: Buddhism, Hinduism and Islam. Somehow, the religion that he grew up hearing about in his childhood was disconnected from the true Jesus. When he was a child, Josh was taught mainly about "following the rules," not about having a meaningful relationship with Jesus and inviting him to be Lord and leader of Josh's life.

"We have to remember to pray to the Lord to stop the forest fires in Fort McMurray," boomed the preacher. Denise's brother, Tim, had been one of the eighty thousand folks who had to be evacuated from Fort Mac. He had managed to keep his job in the oil industry, despite Josh having lost his a year ago. It wasn't surprising since management positions (like Josh's) were always the first ones on the chopping block, before frontline workers. Tim was quite the partier, too. Between all the women, booze and dancing he did, it's a wonder he was able to keep his job. Right now, though, the focus was on getting people like Tim to safety and help them get rooves over their heads., Those folks affected by the fire needed all the prayer they could get!

Pastor Duddley led the congregation in a responsive prayer with cues on the PowerPoint slides. As Josh prayed, though he was no expert, he was sincere in his heart, and he felt a reassuring presence, which must have been God.

"I now would like to invite anyone who would like to come forward and accept Jesus Christ in their heart," proclaimed Duddley. Josh wasn't expecting this, but it seemed as if there were a physical tug that was encouraging him to respond. It seemed to flow from the topic of the sermon—the pastor had been speaking on Zacchaeus trying to get a glimpse of Jesus, and how we ought to be eager, and looking, to find Jesus in our own lives.

The reality was that Josh had never made a personal decision and commitment to accept the Lord into his heart. He had never confessed he was a sinner in need of a Saviour. Now, without a doubt, with Denise praying by his side, he made a fervent commitment to Jesus. Josh repeated the prayer that Duddley led the congregation in, for those who were not yet Christian, and Josh acknowledged that as a sinner, he needed Jesus to come into his heart and forgive him of all his sin, to be his leader for all time.

Then, after wiping off tears of joy from his face, he felt like a heavy weight was taken off of his shoulders. He reached for his Kleenex and blew his nose, composing himself. Then, unbeknownst to Denise, Josh opened up a tiny box, exposing a gleaming ring he had carefully selected and tucked away in his pocked ahead of time. Josh sensed the timing was right. Mustering up all the sincerity he had, Josh got down on one knee and asked Denise to marry him.

"Of course I will, honey!" By now both Denise and Josh were gushing with tears and embraced each other tenderly.

***

Josh could hardly believe it. His new-found religion was not dry or stale at all—it was a vibrant relationship with the Creator of the universe. The very God who knit him together in his mother's womb.

This new relationship with Jesus compelled Josh to be thankful–it was even more exciting than his forthcoming marriage. This pushed him to serve the Lord. He remembered a few short months ago when he frequented the local Edmonton soup kitchen on a regular basis with his young family. Now, with his life transformed by Jesus Christ, Josh wanted to be on the other side of the counter and give back to his community, to see others come to know the same Saviour that Josh had come to believe in.

So, although the Kelowna soup kitchen was run by a secular community centre, Josh still found plenty of opportunities to share the Gospel with people who attended. Josh even gave away some of the Gideons New Testament Bibles that a friend from church had given him. It was such a wonderful experience to be able to lead others to Christ and to see real lives transformed, over time. Not every person Josh shared his faith with got saved, but some of them received Jesus into their hearts. Some of these men that Josh befriended turned from the ravages of pornography, alcohol addiction and eating disorders, turning over new leaves, made alive by new birth into the family of God.

A recent convert himself, Josh was thankful that he was able to follow the Great Commission in *making disciples* and *teaching them to obey* the Lord's teachings. It helped that Josh had grown up in a Baptist home—it was a like a homecoming when Josh came to the Lord, in a sense—as he became reacquainted with all of the theological concepts that he had previously forced into the furthest recesses of his memory.

Josh felt like the prodigal son who had returned to his father after having wandered in the spiritual wilderness of the Sinai Desert for years on end. Thankfully, men in Josh's church were able to disciple Josh, since he was just starting out on his Christian pilgrimage. The Life Group that Josh was a part of met on a weekly basis, rotating among different homes to study the Bible and apply it to the lives of those who attended. In addition, the small group of men were devoted to challenging each other by undertaking service projects in the community, whether it was helping single parents, visiting shut-ins or assisting the elderly with basic household chores. This gave numerous opportunities to carry out the admonition in 1 Peter 3:15 to "Always be prepared to give an answer to everyone who asks you to give the reason for the hope that you have…with gentleness and respect."

Chapter 7

It didn't seem like a manly thing to do: marriage preparation. And this was Josh's second time getting married. The first time, he was in a hurry. He barely knew his then-bride, Lizzy, having only dated her for a few short months before the marriage. The two had nearly married at city hall but then learned of an opening at the local church.

Enough said. Lizzy was a bright, good-looking blond woman with amazing features. Also a native of Newfoundland like Josh, she had followed him all the way to Alberta to start a life there together with him. The two had met each other while attending the College of the North Atlantic in Stephenville back on the East Coast. Josh had studied software development, and Lizzy had studied web development, but when the economy went bust with the dot-com bubble, Josh couldn't find a stable enough job to provide for his family. With the mounting popularity of working in the oil industry out West, Josh's parents encouraged him to go there in pursuit of gainful employment. With Lizzy in tow, Josh took the plunge; each partner wondering if this whole marriage thing would work out between the two of them.

Things went south fairly quickly from the get-go, though. The fact that they had married young and started a family so quickly added to the stress, but their careers also pulled them in separate directions. Not to mention the fact that Lizzy was a staunch atheist, and at that point, Josh had no firm footing when it came to his faith, having backslid and wandered from the faith. Their work schedules also conflicted. Lizzy worked long hours at the web design firm in Edmonton, rising to the position of account executive, with three young children at home. Thank goodness Lizzy's parents were there to help her raise her daughters. At the same time, Josh was gone most of the week, living in a small flat with a couple of other guys up in the party town of Fort Mac. These factors all combined to make Josh's marriage challenging.

So now Denise and Josh were busy preparing for the wedding and overseeing the decorating of the massive church. Josh couldn't care less about the flowers—he just wanted Denise to be happy. The sound system, on the other hand, was critical and needed to be working properly. Ayden and Percy, good church friends, were busy testing the mikes.

The marriage ceremony was being held at a beautiful United Church in Coquitlam…Josh and Denise had some extended family and friends close by, so they didn't have to spend too much money on hotels. Thankfully, Josh had a jobsite nearby too, and Denise managed to snag some time off of work for a few days, which made everything less stressful.

"1-2," Ayden spat into the mike.

"1-2," echoed Patrick on the other side of the sanctuary with another mike. While the couple had more money than Josh had when he entered his first marriage, they certainly weren't loaded, and everything from the sound system to the buffet dinner in the basement was being run on a budget. The fact that Josh had three children contributed, in large part, to the fact that his money was tight.

What Josh still couldn't figure out was how the Syrian refugee fundraiser attendees were going to file out of the basement in time for the four o'clock dinner next Saturday. He knew it was for a good cause, but the lunchtime fundraiser was scheduled on the exact same day as the wedding. The church had raised $60,000 toward sponsoring two refugee families.

Josh could hardly believe the effort and coordination that the Canadian government had undertaken to move such massive amounts of refugees into Canada. The Canadian Border Services Agency, Citizenship and Immigration Canada, and Global Affairs Canada, to name a few, along with Transport Canada's logistical support, were all needed to ensure a seamless transition of newcomer refugees. Josh was truly proud of his country. It was noble to come to the succour of people fleeing such a brutal regime, which persecuted Christians and other minorities throughout the Middle East.

***

Ashleigh, Jenna and Jordan were looking their finest. Jordan was a flower girl, and her two older siblings were bridesmaids.

As Denise walked down the aisle, with her long wedding train behind her and glamorous veil, she was a sight to behold. Although Josh was not a Christian when he first met Denise, he was appreciative that he wasn't intimate with her before marriage. It was something that the Christian marriage counsellor had advised, and it made a difference.

Pastor Duddley looked pretty handsome. His was clean-shaven with his hair slicked back, and he was wearing his best suit. Josh was wearing a tuxedo with a black bow tie.

"Today, it is my honour to join these two special young people in holy wedlock. I had the pleasure of meeting them only a few short months ago. It has grown into a true friendship. I am so thrilled that Josh recently made a commitment to the Lord and was just baptized last week. Praise God!"

The sun was streaming in, glistening off of the multicoloured stained-glass windows on either side of the expansive building. Josh thought back to the first time he met Denise. It was shortly after his breakup with Lizzy. They were at a Second Cup in Alberta. Back in 2014, it would seem that Josh was at the height of his career in the oil industry. He was a manager making a six-figure salary, and he was getting ready to buy a newly built custom home that was by most standards fairly opulent. It had a central staircase in the entranceway and illustrious landscaping, located just south of Fort Mac. He couldn't go through with the purchase when he lost his job.

Duddley cleared his throat. "Marriage is a serious undertaking. It should not be taken lightly. Hebrews 13:4 states, 'Marriage should be honoured by all, and the marriage bed kept pure, for God will judge the adulterer and all the sexually immoral.'" At this point, some of the non-Christians in the room were starting to feel uncomfortable. But he pressed on, unabated.

"Though you have gone through several weeks of marriage counselling, nothing prepares you for the real thing. There are real challenges when living life with another sinful person. But don't forget the joys of marriage. Children are a blessing, if you have them, and the union of man and woman is meant to reflect Christ's humble servant-leader relationship with the church, his bride.

"With that context, I ask you, Joshua Walter McConnell, will you take Denise to be your lawfully wedded wife, to love and honour, from this day forward, as long as you both shall live?"

"Absolutely." Josh's face was beaming, with a tear gently rolling down one of his cheeks.

"Very well. Do you, Denise Elaine Patterson, take Joshua to be your lawfully wedded husband, to hold and to cherish from this day forward, as long as you both shall live?"

"I do." Tears were streaming down Denise's face.

"Well, as a minister of the Word of God, and by the powers vested in me by the powers of the Province of British Columbia, I now declare you husband and wife," beamed Pastor Duddley. "What God hath joined together let no man put asunder."

***

A week after the wedding, Josh and Denise were enjoying a group camp with the Cub Scouts. It was a special time when even parents could come up to camp and enjoy all the fun with the Beavers, Cubs, Scouts, Venturers and even a couple of Rovers. The location was at a beautiful campground close to Vernon, BC. Josh knew the Scouting program did exciting activities, such as hiking in the Adirondack Mountains, which were the tallest peaks in the northeastern United States, and exploring the Cabot Trail in Nova Scotia, an outing that Josh participated in on a yearly basis when he was a Scout and Venturer.

There was a famous tale that was passed down to Josh from some old Scouters he knew growing up about a young Venturer who got lost on the descent down Algonquin Peak in the Adirondack Mountains. Josh was glad that this had never actually happened to him. Apparently, the peaks could be very cold at the summit, with arctic-like conditions. This particular Venturer thought he would freeze to death if he did not soon descend the side of the mountain—he had no time to wait for his fellow Scout compatriots. The Venturer in question had clearly violated the regulation of not stepping on the special moss that grew only in the Arctic and at the summit of some of these big peaks.

The good news of this story was that the Venturer was accompanied down the hill by a family of friendly travellers, only to be met up by the groups's leader who had helped locate the missing youth thanks to a park warden.

"Can I go to CJ'17?" Jenna asked, with a whining tone. Her father and stepmother had just finished a satisfying spaghetti dinner. Denise lovingly had her arm around her new hubby. Jenna was only a year younger than Ashleigh, so she'd qualify to go to the next Jamboree in Halifax. Out of all the girls, Jenna was the most excited about anything to do with Scouting. She liked the idea of being paid to be a Scouter, like in the United States, and maybe she'd move there some day to pursue that career option. Jenna had spent most of the weekend enthusiastically practising the Cub law, promise and motto, to the point where Josh and Denise were even starting to get agitated about it.

Before Josh could get out an answer, Ashleigh and Jordan both piped up.

"Can I join Guides next year?"

"I wanna join Beavers!"

Josh looked briefly at Denise with a quizzical look, as though they could afford those luxuries.

"Sure," quipped Denise, without giving the matter any serious thought. She knew about the No One Left Behind program offered by Scouts Canada for low-income families. If the McConnell family couldn't afford Scouting activities for all their children, she was certain that they would qualify for this program. Groceries and the rent were definitely more of a priority than Scouts, but Denise was thankful that organizations had bursaries for folks who were trying desperately to make ends meet and yet wanted to have their children experience the wonder of Scouting.

"Well, you know you'll have to fundraise a lot," suggested Josh, trying to find the right place to roast his marshmallow in the fire so that he could make a delectable s'more. Josh knew some other youth who had gone to Jamborees in the past that were held in Sweden and Japan. There were always intensive fundraisers, from car washes to bake sales to talent show evenings—you name it, they did it.

"I can't wait to see the *Bluenose!*" pipped up Jenna. The *Bluenose* schooner, which had been used for racing, had become synonymous with Halifax, and more generally, Nova Scotia. It was a beauty and was popular enough to be printed on the back of Canadian dimes.

Josh smiled, filled with gratitude. The whole family had enjoyed a thoroughly eventful, sunny day with the Scouts, participating in a rotation of captivating stations. One station built fires, another practised knots (Denise despised doing knots); yet another station taught Cubs about the proper use and handling of stoves when on a camping trip. The stove station was Josh's responsibility. He always loved cooking, especially on camping trips. He had a special gift of taking even the most mundane foods and making them more exquisite to the palate. Denise, on the other hand, was happy to shepherd the Cubs around to the various stations, breaking up any conflict that might escalate between the children.

Coming up that evening was a formal campfire with other Scout groups from the area that were camping at the same time. This was sure to be a rip-roaring time of fun and laughter. All members of the Scout program in attendance were asked to prepare a skit, a song and a cheer. Jenna was excited about doing "the box skit" with her lair. In this skit, the punch line came when the manager of the factory discovered that the workers were making actual cardboard boxes and not products that would be *packed* in the boxes.

Jenna's Cub pack had tons of events that were going to be jam-packed in the next few months, which she planned on attending, including multiple camps. The winter camp that happened at the end of January was located in a charming, secluded cabin on the backside of Kamloops. At that camp, the Cub Scouts learned the essential skills of what to do in the event of an emergency, like blow your whistle three times or put out three bright pieces of clothing in an open space to signal distress to passing airplanes, and how to build snow *quinzhees*. These fascinating shelters provided warmth during the winter months to all who slept in them. The Cubs and Scouters went for long, exhilarating hikes to see the snow-covered mountains, and the weather turned out to be glorious.

In a couple of weeks, the Cub pack was going to plant Scoutrees to help beautify a conservation area north of Kelowna. Another activity that always garnered a strong following was the Jamboree on the Trail—a worldwide movement in Scouts with each group hiking in various locations around the world. Josh's girls enjoyed collecting the crests for all of these excursions and even asked Denise to sowed them onto their campfire blankets; the badges were like trophies that they collected over the years.

Chapter 8

Calvin Hobbs was the coolest employee at Bennett Solar. The coolest employee after Bennett and Josh, of course. Blond hair, blue eyes: Calvin had the makeup of a male model. With a sleek physique and a rugged five o'clock shadow, he had a penchant for spiking up his blond hair every morning in a purposefully disheveled look. Hobbs was just short of six feet and weighed a muscular 185 pounds.

Having risen quickly through the ranks of the fledgling company at Bennett Solar, Hobbs was quickly becoming not only the main technical whiz behind the company, but also the main driver of sales and profit. This was an essential role to fulfill as the company could not survive without growth. Although the technology of connecting solar panels to buildings was relatively straightforward, it was the intricacy of technical skills that was of the utmost importance. Just as each human was different, so too was every building, which required a variety of skills and strategies in order to successfully install the solar panels.

At merely thirty years old, Hobbs still had his whole career in front of him. He looked forward to making a big impact in the renewable energy industry. As a native of Burnaby, BC, Hobbs had studied mechanical engineering for his undergraduate, then for his master's and PhD he had examined the practical, commercial application of alternative energy, in the form of solar power. Before coming to Bennett Solar, he worked for a couple of start-up hydrogen fuel cell companies in the West Coast. He also worked for a stint on the bourgeoning Ottawa light rail. The latter was an exhilarating experience, using more civil engineering skills on the job, the pay was great and the subcontractor that hired him was glad that he had technical know-how and could interpret engineering drawings. This maxim was true: the main skill of any engineer was the ability to solve *problems*, and Hobbs did this with resolve.

    Right now Hobbs was hundreds of feet in the air in a chopper approaching Fort McMurray. Josh McConnell accompanied him. Both he and Josh were on vacation volunteering with the Red Cross in an effort to help with the Alberta fire crisis. The whole province was in chaos. And yet, Canadians had really banded together in a phenomenal way. Dozens of organizations and companies big and small across the country were pitching in to help with relief efforts.

    Their pilot, Jean-Luc Ladouceur, used to be a farmer in north Regina, Saskatchewan. Born in Churchill, Manitoba, to a Métis family, he had a heavy French accent. Having farmed a two-hundred-acre mixed-purpose farm for over twenty-five years, he decided to become a pilot. Ladouceur looked back with fondness on his farming career—he recalled the recent grain crisis, which resulted in fines being introduced by Parliament to get the grain moving with CP and CN rail during the long, cold winter of 2013 and 2014.

As the three men were flying high in the sky, over the charred buildings and the abandoned homes, Josh was profoundly thankful that no one had died in the traumatic forest fire that had ravaged Fort McMurray. He was immensely thankful that so many generous, kind-hearted Canadians had rallied around this community, including Edmontonians, who had welcomed into their homes many families fleeing the flames.

Josh was immensely happy for all that the Lord had sovereignly orchestrated in his own life. He had struggled terribly, in silence, with a secret pornography addiction for many gruelling years. The internet, having become more ubiquitous since the early 2000s, did not make matters better. In fact, it made matters worse. Yet Josh was grateful for the Celebrate Recovery program, which had helped him break free of his addiction, thanks to the life-changing gospel of Jesus Christ. Josh rested confidently knowing that the Lord gave him the strength daily to have an abundant, God-glorifying life in him. Only in Christ could Josh do all things and abate the flesh, which warred against his body.

When they had reached maximum altitude, Josh checked his phone to remind himself of the date today. It was Victoria Day, or May Two-Four weekend. As Josh cruised two hundred feet in the air, he thought of all the Fort McMurray inhabitants who would be ordinarily cracking opening cases of beer and spending quality time with friends and family, a welcome repose in chock full, hectic schedules. He wondered why Canada still celebrated Victoria Day when most of its citizens probably had no clue about the significance of Queen Victoria as it pertained to their country's history.

It was certainly true that many Commonwealth countries celebrated monarchs' birthdays, but how many Canadians actually celebrated Queen Victoria's role in establishing Canada? Josh figured that in the US, President's Day and the Fourth of July had deeper significance for Americans than Victoria Day had for Canadians. Perhaps it was a lack of patriotism or a case of being ill-informed when it came to Canada's history, but most Canadians were more interested in opening up their cottages and enjoying a few fireworks than considering how the queen had selected Ottawa as the nation's capital.

Josh reflected on how European countries celebrated their royals: *Koningsdag*, or King's Day, in the Netherlands, Trooping the Colour festivities in England, to name a couple. It always seemed that other nations had more nationalistic fervour than Canada. If only they taught in the school system more about Canada's roots, more about the country's history, thought Josh. But, then again, other Commonwealth countries, such as Australia, had considered severing their association with the British monarchy.

The other popular Canadian activity on the May Two-Four weekend was the start of the summer planting season. Josh remembered planting tomato seeds one year in late April at his home in Edmonton, and it was a disaster. It saddened Josh's heart to know that the simple seasonal pleasure of planting a vegetable garden would not be something Fort McMurray residents could do for a little while. But that was why he was here with Hobbs doing what they could on their vacation, helping the battered community to get back on its knees.

Hobbs, Josh and Ladouceur landed on some rocky terrain just outside of Fort McMurray. As the group joined a first aid team to help provide basic services to the residents who were fleeing the area, Josh could see a few elderly folks close to a burnt-out building, tugging what remained of their possessions. All they had was stuffed in a rusted bundle buggy. Josh saw that they were Indigenous locals—a husband and wife. The recent tragedies in Attawapiskat came to mind. Offering up a silent prayer to God for all Indigenous people in the country, Josh pleaded with the Lord to remember those who were struggling with suicide, alcoholism and broken families—partially resulting from the residential school system.

Josh thought of his friend, who was involved in helping the Cree, the youth especially, in northern Quebec. What a worthy cause to devote one's time to! If only he could get involved in serving these communities to the degree that his friend, Fred, had committed. Josh made a mental note that in the next little while, he would volunteer with a ministry giving hope to Indigenous people.

Chapter 9

Once Josh had given first aid to the elderly people by the burnt-out five-story office building, Hobbs and Ladouceur set up a water station close by. The team had granola bars on hand, which was a great way to give people a much needed energy boost if they hadn't eaten for a while.

As Josh looked up at the parked helicopter, he felt deep gratitude for all of the men and women who diligently served in Canada's military. Of course, these people weren't nameless and faceless strangers to him. Some of Josh's acquaintances from high school had signed up for the Air Force and flew CF-18 Hornets during Operation IMPACT in Iraq, while other friends from college enlisted in the navy.

It wasn't just Josh's high school mates, though. Much of his family had served in the military. Both of Josh's grandfathers had proudly served overseas during the Second World War. Grandpa Bob and the whole McConnell clan were originally from Ireland and had come to Canada during the 1845 potato famine. Josh's maternal grandfather, Stephen, also served in the Second World War. He had flown Lancaster bombers over Bremen, Germany, in the early 1940s, during the heat of the war. Stephen, apparently, was a starred pilot and had won the Victoria Cross.

Grandpa Bob and Papa Stephen were honoured to have come to the aid of Canada when duty called—when Hitler *needed* to be stopped. These grandfathers were part of "the greatest generation," having grown up with the challenges of the Great Depression and then gone on to fight the atrocities of the Second World War. Josh's grandparents had witnessed the remarkable shift in the twentieth century from the age of the horse-and-buggy to the age of the automobile. While Josh had grown up to see the Great Recession and the birth of the Information Age, his grandparents experienced arguably a greater change in their lifetime as society rapidly became more consumeristic, materialistic and increasingly suburban.

One of Josh's great-grandfathers served in the First World War, and a distantly relative on his mother's side took part in the War of 1812. Still, other relatives were involved in William Lyon Mackenzie's rebellion in Upper Canada from 1837–1838. It made for great family stories growing up, everyone huddled around the burning hue of the woodstove. Josh and his many siblings would sip hot cocoa in front of the hearth while his grandparents, aunts and uncles would exchange stories about days gone by and would sing Acadian folk songs. These tunes were not unlike the Cajun melodies of the Bayou.

By the crumbled office building, amid all the debris, Josh, Hobbs and Ladouceur assisted a young couple with a badly dehydrated baby, along with a few hungry teens who had gathered near them. They provided the baby with medical attention and handed out food packages to the latter, bringing their volunteering to a conclusion.

Ladouceur started up and then revved the helicopter engine. "You know, it's a crying shame what happened with the Avro Arrow," he opined, out of the blue.

"You think so?" Hobbs piped up. He was really too young to have understood the gravitas of the cancelled airplane project.

"Absolutely," Josh agreed with Ladouceur on the matter. "My dad and grandpa used to talk about it all the time. Rumour had it that a family member of ours actually assembled the components for a few of the models."

"To think that the Canadian government stopped the project and that any evidence of the aircraft was destroyed without a trace," Ladouceur said, with disgust, as he steered the helicopter up and over charred trees that eventually turned into a lush evergreen forest on their way back to Edmonton. You could see his face turning red as he discussed the Avro Arrow.

"It's like the government is covering up UFOs or something…weird stuff." Hobbs got his two cents in.

Josh adjusted his headset. "You got that. But it's a pity that so many of our national gems have fallen by the wayside as they have either faced bankruptcy or were gobbled up by large multinational conglomerates: Nortel, Stelco, Falconbridge, and the list goes on…" His voice trailed off a wee bit as he looked outside.

Hobbs nodded his head, not sure if his friends could see him or were paying attention. He had always loved the idea of flying helicopters or airplanes, but since he finally got his licence two years ago, he hardly had the time to go out flying. It must have been the fact that they had a couple of young kids at home.

It would be a few minutes still before the three amigos landed just outside Edmonton to drop off the helicopter for refuelling. What a gorgeous day it was, with the sun streaming in. Some of the sky, however, had daunting cloud cover.

"At least Canada still has a few great companies left—think BlackBerry and Bombardier." Ladouceur had a determined look on his face as he put on his sunglasses. He almost looked like a Mr. Potato Head with his stick moustache, horn-rimmed shades and bulbous nose.

"I just hope we can hold onto them. I don't believe you can simply blame the disappearance of big Canadian companies on globalization alone. Switzerland and Sweden both have lots of great companies, and they're not too big population-wise." Josh cracked open a can of pop. He was starting to get tired and was hoping the caffeine jolt from a diet Pepsi would give him energy to get him through to the next leg of his journey.

***

"Ladouceur, this is Bennett, over." The crackling sound of Jimmy Bennett's voice over the aging helicopter radio system startled everyone in the cockpit.

"I can hear you loud and clear, over." Ladouceur adjusted the volume to make sure Bennett wasn't coming in too loud. "It's funny…we were just talking about Canadian success stories, and I'm confident Bennett Solar falls in that category."

"I suppose, especially now that we're developing our new, innovative solar panels with greater energy retention and efficiency in-house," said Josh.

You could hear Bennett let out a garbled chuckle on the other end.

"In-house, yes, but several of the parts are manufactured in China and Mexico," corrected Hobbs, who was actively involved in the development of the new product.

"We're manufacturing as much of them as we can in Canada, without losing money," offered up Josh, who also knew a great deal about how the company was run, as he was on the front line installing solar panels every day. Another factor that had eliminated homegrown manufacturing jobs was the insanely low price of oil.

"I'm impressed with your company," admitted Ladouceur. "We should reach Edmonton in about five minutes."

Chapter 10

After their trip volunteering with the Red Cross, the three compadres disembarked onto the helipad, which was located just outside Edmonton. They were deep in conversation about Canada's identity. Ladouceur, now pushing fifty, was still quite strong and did the heavy lifting when it came to unloading the leftover supplies from the helicopter.

"You know, I'm concerned that Canada's losing its way as a peacekeeper," Hobbs conceded.

"How so?" quipped Josh.

"Well, just take the Balkans and Israel as examples. We no longer have peacekeepers in Bosnia, and in Israel we've scaled back our involvement since the Yom Kippur War."

"Maybe that's because there's simply not as much need for peacekeepers as there was in the past."

Canada was a "middle power." It did not have the military prowess and capacity of the United States, but it was big enough to lend a hand to its neighbour to the south, when it was in agreement with their policy. In other words, Canada was more powerful than smaller countries like Lithuania or Latvia—once proxy states of the vast Soviet Empire—but Canada didn't wield the power of the United States or Russia or even the United Kingdom, France or Germany. Canada knew how it felt to be subservient to the British Empire—we never put up a fight, and we knew what it meant to achieve freedom peaceably as our own sovereign country, back in 1867. In fact, it was only in 1931, with the passing of the Statute of Westminster, that Canada was officially granted its independence.

"I think that the world has fundamentally changed in the twenty-first century," Ladouceur stated emphatically, while unloading the final piece of gear and closing the hatch to the helicopter. "Nowadays, we need a more robust framework than mere peacekeepers. Many of the conflicts are not solvable by simply sending a few Blue Helmets to the proverbial green line. Conflicts are grittier, enemies are clearer and we're seeing more and more actors that simply aren't playing by the rules of the game, like ISIS, for example. The Arab Spring starting in 2011 or Hamas are other examples of dissidents in societies who can't be stopped by peacekeepers."

"I think it's fair to say that we've learned some from Rwanda," Hobbs interjected as the three men headed toward the parking lot. "Lieutenant-General Roméo Dallaire describes a lot of the personal lessons he gleaned in his book *Shake Hands with the Devil*. He has done some real admirable work trying to solve the problem of child soldiers and stopping landmines in countries around the world. I agree with Dallaire: we would be more effective as a nation if we enforced *peacemaking* rather than *peacekeeping*."

Ladouceur had to part ways to get the next helicopter refuelled in time for his next client. But the other two men jumped into the Dodge Durango and headed to the Edmonton airport to catch their flight back to Kelowna.

"It strikes me," started off Josh, "that lately we *have* seen a more aggressive, assertive Canada played out on the international stage. I mean, our whole role in Afghanistan in the early 2000s was one of greatly weakening the Taliban and fighting terror rather than keeping the peace.

"Harper seemed to be more of a hawk as he upped the ante of the Canadian status quo via Operation IMPACT when combating ISIS. Not to mention all the talk of establishing Canadian sovereignty in the Arctic."

"Wait now, before we move on to the topic of Canada's North" Hobbs said as he pulled the Durango into the airport parking lot. "You can't neglect the fact that Canada had moved into a 'rebuilding' role in Afghanistan."

"I know, but you just said it: *moved into*. Initially, we were there in full force, punching more than our weight."

"True. As for the North, I don't know how much skin Canada has in determining who owns what up there. I know the northern countries have until 2018 to make their cases for the Arctic in front of the international committee, but let's be honest: Russia's being superaggressive with all of its fighter jets flying in the Arctic. They think they can stake a big portion of it with their supposed ownership of the Lomonosov Ridge—as well as the Mendeleev Ridge. The

United States, on the other hand, has been arguing since the 1960s that the Northwest Passage is in international waters. It's all about tourism and oil—natural resources. Global warming has certainly accelerated this whole discussion."

Hobbs and Josh had no time to waste. They had a six o'clock flight to catch back to Kelowna. The two men scrambled to get through airport security but inevitably found themselves delayed with additional baggage checks.

After security had done their thing, Josh was interrupted by a phone call. It was Denise making sure everything was okay. "I gotta run, darling!" Josh said firmly, as he and Hobbs ran to their flight terminal. I have to admit, though, he thought, it was refreshing to hear my sweetheart's voice.

Chapter 11

Josh had decided that during the second part of his vacation, he would spend some quality time with his children. And, since he had not yet officially had a honeymoon with Denise, he loved the idea of taking the time to also connect with his lovely bride. It was decided that they would travel to Ontario, along with the children, for a fun-filled canoe trip! This was the first time Josh had taken his girls—all four of them—on a camping experience. So that week, the family flew into Ottawa to begin their vacation together.

There were so many routes from which to choose! After all, Canada was home to an incredibly high amount of the world's freshwater—20 percent. Ontario alone, after all, was bigger than many European countries. A few of Josh's friends from college had grown up in the province and had gone on several internationally recognized expeditions: the gorgeous Baron River canyon, the Groundhog River, the Petawawa River. For a short while, Josh was considering canoeing the French River, which was beautiful, but it had too many cottages and motorboats on it. Also, there wasn't really any whitewater along it.

Josh was looking for a little bit of adventure on the trip. That's why he chose the Temagami River. It was just the right combination of whitewater and more boring parts. Also, Josh had always loved the tall, windswept white pines that were synonymous with Northern Ontario. He could see how the landscape had greatly inspired Tom Thomson of the Group of Seven painters. The canoe trip was planned to start at the river's source: Lake Temagami. Then the river flowed into River Valley, where the mighty Sturgeon River intersected. Josh loved being in this area, where loggers had traditionally gone through, and which had a rich heritage, populated mainly with French settlers.

The five vacationers were going to employ a couple of newly acquired ABS canoes, rented from a local outdoors shop. Although he appreciated cedar strip canoes for flat water, Josh was glad that he was not running them down Class I and II rapids on their upcoming trip. Josh had packed plenty of freeze-dried food; Bennett had loaned him his dehydrator. The idea of having wanigans with tumplines, as were common during historical canoe expeditions, was also appealing, but not practical in whitewater. The "old-fashioned" part of the trip for Josh and his family was going to be that they would cook over an open fire, just as Josh had learned from his younger years in the Scouting program, and from his father.

When they first started the trip, the weather was spectacular. It was a little on the hot side with thirty-two-degree weather plus humidex. Denise and Jordan especially made sure to get lots of swim breaks in. By day three, there were nasty storm clouds on the horizon. With the overcast weather came a welcomed current of cooler air that was refreshing after the earlier intense heat. On their first portage, as Josh was making sure his family got all their gear on their backs and was getting one of the canoes on his shoulders, Josh reflected on Bill Mason and the legacy he left Canadians when it came to the art of canoe tripping.

Josh had read several of Bill Mason's books over the years and was fascinated by the man. It was intriguing how a small, humble man had had such a profound impact on Canadian culture. Especially unique were the videos that Mason produced in collaboration with the National Film Board. Those were the days, Josh pondered silently to himself. Although documentary films ranged in their quality, often coming off as cheap or low budget, Bill's videos were authentic and heartfelt. Another dimension of Mason's life was how the canoeist would often escape the pressures of life by going on solo canoe trips in the wilderness, along all the famous—and sometimes infamous—Canadian canoe routes. Not unlike former prime minister Pierre Elliott Trudeau, Bill Mason would draw strength and inspiration from the wilderness, whether it be by himself or with a friend.

There was also a spiritual element woven into Mason's forays into the wilderness. Mason's relationship with God was reflected in his connection to nature. He could see God's handiwork in the trees, in the water; the wildlife all around him was a testament to the Almighty. This resonated with Josh. Faith wasn't meant to stay in a box, reserved exclusively for Sunday mornings. No, our faith affected every part of our lives, and we were commanded as Christians to "go and make disciples of all nations, baptizing them in the name of the Father and of the Son and of the Holy Spirit, and teaching them to obey everything I have commanded you" (Matthew 28:19–20). This was the call. This was the top-priority mission for every Christian, whether they be overseas missionaries or emissaries in the marketplace.

Enjoying nature with his family was a way for Josh to be actively discipling his family and drawing them into a deeper relationship with Jesus Christ. Although plagued at times by doubt, Josh knew there had to be a Creator God because of the purity of nature. Josh was reminded of the Scripture: "For since the beginning of the world God's invisible qualities—his eternal power and divine nature—have been clearly seen, been understood from what has been made, so that people are without excuse" (Romans 1:20).

***

Josh carefully put down his canoe. The portage was not long, but it was midafternoon, and he was hoping to have his family reach their site soon so they could set up camp. He had to return to pick up just one more load of gear before continuing on along the river.

Ashleigh and Jordan were already showing signs of fatigue. Or was it laziness? Jenna somehow continued along her merry way as she helped move gear along the second portage. "This is so much fun!!" she exuded, with Denise trailing not too far behind, carrying a couple of tents and stray life jackets. As Josh headed back to pick up the final load, dripping with sweat, he gave Denise a peck on the cheek as he crossed her along the path.

The sun came out. The temperature warmed only slightly. Josh could see the sun dancing in the shimmering leaves. A hint of autumn was in the air, though it was only the end of June. Even though he relished summer vacations, Josh longed for the cooler weather and gorgeous colours that the fall brought. He also hated the mosquitoes that were deadly around this time of year—at dawn and at dusk. Josh scarfed a quick handful of trail mix, quickly scanning the bilingual label to look at the ingredients, before putting his seventy-five-litre trail pack on. He loved being Canadian. In Europe, they had labels with more than two languages on them. Even in the States, more and more material on packages and websites was being translated into Spanish.

The pack was a little lighter now that he was two days into the trip and a chunk of the food stored in the pack had been consumed. He and Denise had also finished roughly half of their small supply of beer since the beginning of the voyage—the lighter gear certainly helped them move faster!

As Josh started back along the portage again, he was thankful to see Denise yet again along the path. There was still the yellow barrel left with the remaining food in it. He gave the backpack he had been carrying to Denise to carry and then went back a few metres to get the food barrel. As Josh started one more time down the portage trail to join the rest of the girls, he couldn't help but be grateful for the fact that they had a food barrel. He loathed having to hang the food in the trees after dinner. There never seemed to be a tree that was large and solid enough to withstand the weight of the food bag.

One time, when Josh was camping with some university friends, he saw what he thought were raccoons, but possibly were grizzly bears, trying to roll around the barrel with no success. He and his friends had left the barrel near the campfire, a few feet away from their tents. Yet this didn't come close to some of the stories he had heard from his friends when they went camping.

His good buddy, Nate, had told him of an experience he had had camping at a provincial park a number of years ago. When evening had come, none of the campers wanted to put the food away properly. The group was car camping, and all that was needed was to put the food in the coolers that the group had brought and then place the coolers in the minivan. One of the more influential peers had voiced his opinion that the food just need to be tucked in the coolers. No one seemed to offer up a dissenting opinion.

Bad idea! At about eleven that evening, when everyone had settled into their tents, they could hear the raccoons emerging to gorge themselves on their nighttime feast. They all made a very distinctive clucking sound; they could see the baby raccoons enthusiastically run toward their supper, beady eyes and all. In the morning, utter devastation. The peanut butter was destroyed, along with the bread. None of the food that the raccoons had touched could be eaten by humans. It wasn't hygienic in the least—there were bite marks in everything.

***

As Josh reached the end of the third portage, he wiped the sweat off his brow. His do-rag had captured most of the sweat emanating from his balding head. He took another mouthful of granola clusters, and offered some to the rest of his family, but most of them were holding off for lunch.

Once they had been canoeing for a short while, the group eddied into a niche in the river, with spectacular trees jutting out of the side of it. Josh cracked open the pita bag and some kielbasa. He was glad the cheddar had lasted this long, as he had meticulously preserved it in a cheesecloth. The pungent flavour was due to age. Josh had shelled out a small fortune for it at the health food store for his family to appreciate during the trip. He was glad that Denise now made a decent salary as a social worker!

Ashleigh meticulously cut a few chunks of the spiced kielbasa. It was something that Josh didn't normally splurge on and buy at home. Instead, he often opted for tuna fish or salmon. But what the heck, he thought. We may as well be generous to ourselves when we're roughing it.

Jenna took a deep breath of the fresh air that surrounded her. She loved being off for the summer and spending some quality time with her family, happy that her father's divorce was finally over, but sad that her parents couldn't reconcile their differences. Although she excelled at most school subjects, she had a general distain for math and science. Her other two siblings, on the other hand, were cerebral—logical and analytical in their thinking—and aspired to careers in engineering or architecture. Something with lots of calculating involved.

The water glistened, shimmering in all of its elegance and manifold beauty. The five travellers devoured a well-deserved lunch, revelling in the camaraderie. Denise ensured that the girls had their fair share of vegetables: cucumber slices and baby carrots were doled our liberally. They went well, after all, with the hummus and Greek dip. The group had to finish up these dips before they went bad as a result of the hot temperatures.

It was now dessert time, which meant eating parts of a thick, 90 percent dark chocolate bar. Josh divvied up the portions and threw them at each lady.

"This would go down real well with some milk!" Jordan admitted, wishing she could reach into a fridge and have a cold glass of it.

"Well, we only have a bit of coffee cream left. I'm afraid we used up our two percent milk after the second day of our trip," Josh said matter-of-factly.

The group packed up their backpacks and barrel at a leisurely pace. They were in no rush. Josh made sure to keep some dried fruit handy so that everyone would be able to have snacks later on. Denise and Ashleigh started to load the canoes in the water. Once all the gear was packed up and the canoes were in the water, Josh got into his canoe with Jordan and lingered around the miniwaterfall nearby. He carefully pulled out his fishing rod and cast a few lines.

After about a minute, he pulled out a huge walleye, as if it were no trouble at all.

"Wow! That's dinner for tonight," he said. It would be a good addition to the smallmouth bass that Denise had successfully caught earlier in the day.

***

The two-canoe expedition headed down the Temagami River, and everyone was reenergized after their lunch and delighted with the prospect of a yummy dinner of freshly caught fish alongside rehydrated carrots and beans, cooked by campfire. It was fascinating how much of camping revolved around the well-earned meals. Everything tasted better when cooked outside, on the fire.

The map that Josh studied as he paddled, with the assistance of Jenna in the bow, was fairly straightforward and demarcated all of the campsites with an *X* with a flame on top. There was a topographical element to the map, too, accurately showing the various geological gradations of the surrounding landscape. Up ahead there was a borderline Class II rapid that they could barely make out around the curve of the current. Josh stood up carefully in the canoe as he carefully back-paddled to assess the rapid. It looked like they could follow the current easily enough as long as they followed the V-patterns that Josh had identified.

As Josh and Jenna approached the rapids, the water glimmered spectacularly, sparkling as if it were a multifaceted jewel. Josh was thankful that the water level was high this year; it would make their descent down the rapid a lot easier.

After sitting back down in the canoe, Josh paddled ferociously and yelled at Jenna in the front.

"Hard—paddle hard!...Back-paddle! NOW, get your back into it!"

After successfully reaching the end of the rapid, Josh eddied into a natural alcove surrounded by cedar trees. He didn't even try to shout at Denise over the sound of the rapids, but motioned a *c'mon* with his hands, waving the other canoe forward so as to indicate that it was safe to proceed down the rapid.

Denise, squinting to see the motion that Josh had made, with Ashleigh in the bow and Jordan in the middle, started off on a strong note down the rapid. Josh could easily see them all smiles at first; then, all of a sudden, they crashed down the first dip in the rapid. It was exhilarating. Then out of blue, the canoe became unsteady. Denise leaned over to one side ever so slightly to compensate. Next, before the canoeists realized, the boat was thrust over to its side and turned over. Fortunately, everyone was wearing a life jacket and floated along, bobbing up and down in the water along with the gear, until the end of the rapid.

Josh, seeing that everyone looked fine, did not even try to swim up to rescue his girls but instead hurried over to the canoe and gear so that they wouldn't be lost downstream. Having grabbed the canoe, Josh blocked the gear from moving down the river. He scooped up the waterlogged packs, one by one, and deposited them on the nearby shore.

By this point, the girls had all found themselves on dry ground. With Ashleigh's help, Josh righted the vessels by doing canoe over canoe.

"That was fun!" exclaimed Ashleigh.

"Not so much," her sister Jordan admitted, who was completely soaked and didn't have her bathing suit on at the time.

"You know…I got a photo of you all as you came down the rapid." Josh held up his waterproof camera and passed it to Denise to look at the picture before passing it along to the children. They all oohed and aahed over the action shots as they passed the camera to one another.

Everyone made sure to get fully hydrated after they lay the gear on the shore to dry. They shared the dry fruit that Josh had put at the top of the food barrel earlier in the day.

"All right, we need to make hay while the sun is shining," Josh said, trying not to let his enthusiasm wain. It was nearing five o'clock, and the group hadn't yet reached their campsite. Fortunately, the clouds had disappeared somewhat, and the sun was shining through.

The canoes were hurriedly put into the water by Denise and Josh in an effort to get everyone moving faster. Admittedly, the group was moving sluggishly, having been exhausted by the hot temperatures. They had pressed through that part in the afternoon when many vacationers like to take a nap.

This last stretch of the day seemed to go by faster than the first stretch. As Josh followed the map and led the canoe behind him, the convoy made good time, identifying the major landmarks. Josh always seemed to have an innate sense of direction and to know which was north, despite having forgotten to bring a compass. It was great not getting lost! The map made sense, and the campsites, bends in the river and topography were easy enough to identify.

At about six o'clock, the group reached their destination only to find that their campsite was occupied. Darn, thought Denise, as she gazed at Josh and communicated a frustrated, almost frenetic look. The strange thing was that they hadn't seen a lot of travellers or canoeists during their trip thus far, only a few fishermen in motorboats.

Josh was not dismayed. He had a backup campsite up his sleeve and doggedly had his family forge on. The good news was that the next campsite was just around the bend. This alternate site was even better than the one originally picked out, because even though it was slightly more exposed, there was a massive smooth rock for jumping off of and a little nook off to one side that would be perfect for catching fish.

When they reached the site, Josh barked orders at his children about removing the gear from the canoes, while he and Denise lugged the canoes a fair ways up from the shore and turned them upside down. Josh was tempted to tie the canoes up to a couple of nearby trees, but decided it wasn't necessary. The wind was starting to pick up, but it wasn't strong enough to turn over the canoes.

By now, as six-thirty was approaching, the family wanted to set up camp and get some dinner ready. The children tackled the tents—

with some help from Denise—while Josh started preparing the spaghetti and got the fire going. Within twenty minutes the tents were set up, and dinner was well on its way to being finished: all the vegetables were chopped, and the meat sauce and noodles were cooking.

Chapter 12

Thursday, June 30, 7 p.m.

As the McConnell family headed back on the plane, they were all very thankful for a tremendously relaxing holiday. The last leg of their trip had gone relatively hassle-free, with food to spare and no damage to the rented canoes. The outfitter had even given Josh a deal for the next time he wanted to rent canoes.

Josh had almost finished his vacation. Before long, he would be back at work, immersed in the daily grind. But before he returned to work, he was going to fully enjoy the long weekend with his family—it was Canada Day tomorrow!

Before his family trip, he had helped his new friend and work colleague from the IT department, Sanjay Vermasandalaj study for his immigration exam to become a Canadian citizen. Josh was unaware that Canada Day was originally called Dominion Day, up until 1982, in fact. Those who were monarchists were more than a little bit perturbed with the name change. While those who wanted Canada to strike out on its own would have wondered why the name didn't change sooner. That same year of the name change also marked the first year that Canada achieved its autonomy from Great

Britain with the signing of the Canada Act and the repatriation of the constitution.

The relatively young country had come a long way since 1867, when the United Province of Canada joined with New Brunswick and Nova Scotia to pass the British North America Act. This paved the way for the passing of the 1931 Statute of Westminster in the United Kingdom, allowing Canada to achieve independence. Canada generally followed the pattern of *gradualism*, with no big revolutions leading to republics like in France or the United States. Instead, we quietly, peacefully, worked toward full independence, in a mostly tranquil manner.

Then there was the whole issue of fostering national unity. The fact that there were not one but two referendums in Canada on questions of national unity, leading to the country staying together, has been nothing short of a miracle. We solved our differences through consensus. That's what has given us insight into working toward a common goal, and it has made us good peacekeepers.

In a matter of hours, Josh would be enjoying Canada Day with his friends and family under a deep blue, cloudless sky emitting nice and hot temperatures.

***

The previous night had been a tiring one. This morning, in addition to dealing with jet lag, Josh and some of his family felt like they were coming down with something. Now that they were all back in British Columbia, the family was grateful to have gained three more hours of precious sleep.

Kelowna was a booming place, with development growing at a fast clip. Josh had considered trying to scrape together some cash to buy a detached home but had decided on renting a townhome as he settled into his job of installing solar panels. It was easy to rent—no back-breaking or costly renovation work was required. At Josh's Calgary home, he and his friends had completed several big renovations on their houses. They probably weren't all that necessary given that the home was barely ten years old. Nevertheless, it was a challenge that proved to drag on longer than any one of them expected, especially when he was also taking care of his young children.

Josh had planned on having a few friends and family members over in the evening, downing a beer or two, and eating some great barbecued steak and potatoes before the evening festivities and fireworks. Also, Josh's sister was in town visiting from New Brunswick. Maxine was employed in the public relations arm of a large multinational pharmaceutical company.

Meanwhile, during the day, Josh was tidying up the house before his guests arrived. He found some time to indulge in a quick break by working on a Canada Day quiz typed up in *The Daily Courier*. There were so many references to subjects he never knew about Canada. He had to cheat and peek at the answers several times.

For instance, Josh had no clue that William Lyon Mackenzie King was Canada's longest serving prime minister. He had served the country faithfully in the years up to and including the Second World War, despite some downright bizarre activities involving his dog and dead mother. There were so many pearls to discover in Canada's checkered history! Another factoid was that the music of our national anthem was musically composed by Calixa Lavallée, and the lyrics were written by Sir Adolphe-Basile Routhier.

Just as Josh was finishing cleaning the bathroom and quality-checking the kitchen tidy-up that was assigned to his daughters, he heard the doorbell ring. His older sister had arrived earlier than expected. Right behind her, Denise snuck in. She had escaped for the whole day to a spa about an hour away from their home, somehow eschewing the cleaning-up duties in the process.

"So glad to see you!" Maxine, Josh's sister, gave a sloppy kiss as he answered the door. A man who appeared to be her boyfriend stood nervously in the doorway, a buff middle-aged man with angular features and a receding hairline.

Everyone got in and settled on the patio. Maxine's German shepherd, Butch, who had come along to the gathering, wagged his tail and gleefully greeted all those in attendance. The conversation turned quickly to the topic of family. Josh's Grandpa Bob was born northwest of Toronto, grew up in a large family on a farm and became an investment banker. Gramps had quite a knack for real estate, to boot. Try as he may, Grandpa Bob found that he could never really get a good return in the stock market. He read all the books. He listened to all the radio programs. Any newspaper clipping or article in a journal he could lay his hands on was fair game.

But that all changed when Grandpa Bob got serious about focusing on real estate to generate wealth, to the exclusion of the stock market. He had lost a pile of cash when one of the natural resource stocks he invested in went bust with the economy. His pick seemed to be a winner, and he had tried to diversify his portfolio, while still preferring conservative investments such as bonds and utility stocks. Grandpa Bob's whole foray into the world of investments started when he took the money his wife was paid from her discharge from the Woman's Auxiliary Air Force at the conclusion of the Second World War. Originally from a dirt poor family in the shipbuilding city of Aberdeen, Grandma Martha saw her service to Great Britain's war efforts as a way to "escape" from a life of squalor and dire poverty. At any rate, Grandma Martha was demobbed first, before her husband, and the newlyweds ended up using the money she was given for her service to go toward a down payment on a modest home. It was called a "'cherry box home," due to its overall resemblance to the box used to pick fruit.

Over the years, Grandpa Bob had built up a small fortune, not only from his career progression up through the ranks of the bank, but also through renting out rooms in his various houses, buying and selling other rental properties and capitalizing on the market for second mortgages. Bob brokered mortgages and took over homes when the owner defaulted, renting them out for a bit. Then, when the market picked up again, the home in question could be sold again— at a profit. Grandma Martha and Grandpa Bob's children were faithful to help out their parents with the maintenance of the residential properties. The "sweat money" was hard-earned, and over the years, a fortune was amassed.

While Josh didn't rent out houses the way his grandfather did, he did learn a strong Protestant work ethic from his father and grandfather. His other grandfather used to talk about the concept of grace-driven effort, a teaching that the Apostle Paul seemed to promote as well. The idea is that the Christian life is a race to be won, but it is won by focusing on Christ, the author and finisher of our faith, as detailed in the book of Hebrews. Christ has given us his strength, allowing us to say no to ungodly desires and yes to godly desires, escaping the corruption of our faith, as shown in the book of 2 Peter. Godly desires brought about actions such as sharing our faith and making healthy decisions.

***

Josh was happy getting to know John, his sister's boyfriend. He was a personal trainer by profession and was an avid cyclist in his spare time. As Josh was talking to John, he realized how important it was, as a Christian, to nurture friendship, wherever it could be found…and to consider others more highly than himself.

John told his story, in fits and starts, during the conversation about family. A few of Jenna and Jordan's friends were present also for the Canada Day celebrations at the McConnell residence. Ashleigh was over at her best friend's house for a sleepover.

The recounting of John's childhood was interesting. He had come from a troubled home. His parents abused him both physically and verbally; his father had had a serious drinking and smoking problem. When John had his first major relationship, John didn't have any children because he wanted to focus on his career as a fitness trainer. Later on, he also did bodybuilding on the side to earn some more cash. He even earned a couple of medals and awards to prove his skill.

Josh pegged John at about forty years old. His salt and pepper hair gave away the fact that he was middle-aged.

"My dad has been doing much better in the last ten years, when it came to fishing Atlantic salmon and cod…not to mention his health has greatly improved. Despite having to have an artificial larynx, the cancer he had a few years ago hasn't come back, and his liver is in much better condition," reflected John. He was proud of the living his father had eked out in part due to the resurgence of fisheries on the East Coast. In the early 1990s, John's father had gone out west in search of better fishing grounds. He was happy to have returned the East Coast more recently and came to understand the necessity of the Department of Fisheries and Oceans' commercial fishing restrictions.

"You know, it wasn't just the Newfie fishermen who had pushed our fisheries over the edge. It was the French, Spanish and Portuguese that contributed a lot to the depletion of fish in my province," Maxine added with near certainty in her voice, getting her two cents in the conversation. She remembered researching the topic extensively for a project in middle school.

"I hear ya," echoed Denise. "I came from a hard-working fishing family myself. We're from Tofino. My parents were real hard-working folks—from dawn till dusk—fishing mainly halibut, though, some tuna as well. What can I say? They had fifteen children to feed."

"There's always been some fishermen, throughout Canada, who would never play by the rules of the game," chimed in Josh. "Greed settled into their hearts. When you think about it, fishing was the only livelihood available for many of the families on the Atlantic coast."

"It still is," said John. "Sure, there are call centres, government offices and other industries like Irving shipbuilding and deep-sea oil exploration. But then there's fishing. For many people, it's the only livelihood they've ever known. Otherwise, they've had to move elsewhere in Canada or abroad."

"I love the charm and appeal of Newfoundland," remarked Denise wistfully, looking into the distance. "Each area of the province is so unique…it's so diverse, yet unified. Except for St. John's—it's too cosmopolitan—too fast-paced for my liking. It's lost its small-town feeling. But the people, no matter where you go in Newfoundland, are so friendly," she insisted.

"To think, St. John's, the biggest city in Newfoundland, only has a hundred thousand people," Josh pointed out. "I guess Canada has a lot of small cities…and then there's Toronto," he said with a smile. "But I love everything about Newfoundland—the people, the culture, the brightly painted buildings. Makes for touching photographs and calendars."

"And Newfoundland, in its own way, has a culture that is so profoundly different than Nova Scotia and Prince Edward Island. The history, for example, is not the same. Newfoundland was nearly ceded to the Americans—the province relied on the fishing industry in a similar way as in Bostonians. In the end, however, by 1949, the province agreed to join the Confederation of Canada. Joining Canada won out due to the strong connection the Canadians had to England."

Josh offered all of the adults ice-cold beers that had been chilling in the cooler since before everyone arrived. Most accepted, except for Maxine, whohad a glass of Chardonnay she had brought along. After everyone was served, Josh grabbed a chilled Heineken for himself. As munchies were distributed, the conversation turned toward an upcoming round-Canada trip that John and Maxine were planning. The two had been saving up what they could for an exciting trip.

The idea was that they would take the Via Rail train across the country. But first they would start with a flight out to their hometown of Corner Brook, Newfoundland, for a few days. Then they'd fly back to Halifax and take the train to Toronto. From Toronto, the journey would continue west and north to Churchill, Manitoba, then back down south and further west and north again to Prince Rupert. For the last leg of the trip, they would head south and west to Vancouver.

"I think lots of Ontario is kinda boring to travel across…so why travel it by train?" Denise asked matter-of-factly.

"Well, we're going in the fall, and the colours in northwestern Ontario and Manitoba will be just fabulous," John explained.

"Darn right," Maxine quipped. "We may take time at some significant stops to go camping." By the way Maxine was talking, it seemed like she had drunk a little more beer than she wanted to.

"Really? So let me get this straight—you're going to do all this travelling on the train *and* prolong your trip by camping?" Josh questioned his sister, as if he were trying to solve a mystery.

"You got that, Pontiac," John replied, with enthusiasm.

The three adults' banter continued about the future trip, with Maxine and Josh describing such details as what camping equipment they would bring along with them.

Soon enough, darkness descended, and everyone enjoyed the fireworks. Some of the neighbours also joined in the festivities since the McConnells' backyard was sizably bigger than the neighbours'. Having been a scorcher of a day, the night air became less stagnant as the cool air blew gently. Still, the whole area was in need of a good drench. Water levels had been low all summer, and there had been fire bans at all the major provincial campsites. Josh figured it was mainly Vancouver proper that experienced the dreary, wet weather.

Made in the USA
Middletown, DE
17 November 2017